Winter of
the Coup

Center Point
Large Print

Also by Carter Travis Young and available from
Center Point Large Print:

The Savage Plain
Winchester Quarantine
Guns of Darkness

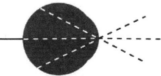

**This Large Print Book carries the
Seal of Approval of N.A.V.H.**

WINTER
of the
COUP

Carter Travis Young

CENTER POINT LARGE PRINT
THORNDIKE, MAINE

This Center Point Large Print edition
is published in the year 2019 by arrangement with
Golden West Literary Agency.

First US edition: Doubleday

The text of this Large Print edition is unabridged.
In other aspects, this book may vary
from the original edition.
Printed in the United States of America
on permanent paper.
Set in 16-point Times New Roman type.

ISBN: 978-1-64358-067-8 (hardcover)
ISBN: 978-1-64358-071-5 (paperback)

Library of Congress Cataloging-in-Publication Data

Names: Young, Carter Travis, author.
Title: Winter of the coup / Carter Travis Young.
Description: Center Point Large Print edition. | Thorndike, Maine :
    Center Point Large Print, 2019.
Identifiers: LCCN 2018046317| ISBN 9781643580678 (hardcover) |
    ISBN 9781643580715 (paperback)
Subjects: LCSH: Western stories. | Large type books.
Classification: LCC PS3575.O7 W498 2019 | DDC 813/.54—dc23
LC record available at https://lccn.loc.gov/2018046317

For Hank and Maggie Bizet,
muy buenos amigos

1

Sometimes a cowpoke could go along year after year without ever hearing more than one name applied to him, other than in a fight. Oakes and Spud, for instance, were simply Oakes and Spud. The first sounded like a surname, the second like a substitute for some Christian name, but no one ever thought of calling Oakes and Spud anything else. Usually in tandem, since these two young waddies generally paired off.

Oakes and Spud were a fun-loving pair, neither one old enough to vote. Hanging on at the Rocking-S for the winter couldn't have meant much to them at all. Lee Crosswhite had a hunch it would have taken little to jog them into lighting a shuck while the dust of the fall roundup was still settling. They had money to jingle, and when that ran out there would always be a woman in Cheyenne or Laramie or way down in Kansas City who would be happy to keep a young, woolly, hard-bodied cowboy fed and warm and contented until spring.

The trouble was that somewhere along the line Oakes and Spud had latched onto the fact that Crosswhite was set on holing up at the Rocking-S to hibernate. Doing him out of the job probably wasn't even their intention. If it was, it was no more to them than a joke. Old Frank Sells, owner of the Rocking-S, kept a string of line camps up on his high range, and he liked to have a man or two up there at each shack all winter. Oakes and Spud wouldn't even last it out. They would go crazy penned up in a little shack together with the snow piling high enough to block out the only window. It took an all-weather hand like Crosswhite to ride out the loneliness and the boredom without getting cabin fever. You would have thought Frank Sells would have seen that, even after what happened.

On the other hand, Crosswhite should have made a quicker guess that Oakes and Spud might be up to one of their jokes, if only for fun, after Sells tabbed him for one of the winter camps.

Sells let Crosswhite pick out an extra horse from the cattleman's remuda, but the pickings by the end of the fall work were lean. There was one big dun-colored mare, a dusty gray with a wickedly rolling black eye, who looked strong enough to pull a plow through rock. The claybank, as a horse of that coloring was often called, was famed for its endurance. Crosswhite had wondered about the mare earlier. Trouble was, no one had been able to break her to the saddle. He decided to give it a try.

They were all out there watching him that first day, Oakes and Spud, Sut Rossiter, Charley Searls and Hank Bannon, Cherokee and the rest of the bunch, but Crosswhite didn't give them any satisfaction. He spent an hour leading the balky claybank around with a bit in her mouth and the unwelcome saddle on her back, talking to her like a lover. Some of the boys took to catcalling and jeering at him, and Sut Rossiter sneered in that way of his, but Crosswhite ignored them. He wasn't out to win the crew over, only that mare. After a while his audience became bored and began to drift away.

Except for Oakes and Spud, who watched, friendly enough, calling out advice now and then or commenting on how the gray's legs looked almost as bent as Lee's did and her jaw just as ornery.

Crosswhite rode her the second day. When he climbed on she simply stood there for about thirty seconds, as if she couldn't believe it. Then she exploded straight up.

Crosswhite had broken enough horsehide to string out for a mile, but in all his time he'd never before wrapped his long legs around a lightning bolt. The big claybank seemed to be able to crack her spine like a whip. She had a little twist at the top of her hump that was enough to shed skin. When that didn't unseat the stubborn human on her back she tried scraping him off along the rails of the corral. Crosswhite got mad at that. He was going to ride that dirty gray mare straight into the pit of hell where she'd been born. Oakes and

9

Spud were right. The set of his jaw was just as mean and stubborn as the mare's.

For nearly a minute he clung to his perch. Then the gray came down on all fours in a jarring landing that broke one of his toeholds. She went straight up again, defying any laws of anatomy, jackknifing with her head down between her front legs so violently that Crosswhite sailed free.

In midair he did a somersault. His back and shoulders slammed into the hard ground ahead of his heels, jarring all the breath out of him. He lay gasping and choking in a cocoon of dust, fighting for wind, thinking that every bone in his body must be broken and hearing the shrieks of laughter through that dusty curtain.

He struggled upward. If that mare was mean enough, she might try to trample him. . . .

His legs wobbled as if the pins had been pulled. Pawing wind tears and dirt away from his eyes, he became aware of a raw patch where his cheek had been scraped.

The claybank was standing aloof on the far side of the corral, watching him with those hostile black eyes. Nearby, Oakes was hanging onto Spud to keep from tumbling off the rail, he was laughing so hard.

Crosswhite walked circles in the corral dust until his legs seemed solid once more. Then he stalked the mare.

On the third try he stayed aboard long enough

for the big horse to tire briefly. After an incredible series of jumps the horse paused, trembling and frothing, her nostrils blowing hard. Crosswhite dismounted quickly.

She wasn't finished, only taking a breather, but neither was he. He just had a hunch she was going to outlast him on this day, and he wanted to quit a winner.

Tomorrow would be different.

Crosswhite never even thought of checking his gear. He was too busy clucking and talking to that dun-colored mare, reminding her that she had failed to throw him on her last try and that that was the way it was going to be from now on and she might as well get used to the idea, like it or not. She didn't seem to mind his being around her as much as she had before, and Crosswhite began to think that this might be easier than he had figured.

He paid little heed to the large crowd that had gathered, not counting it important. And when Spud insisted on helping him keep the mare quiet until she was securely saddled and Crosswhite was safely in place, he was not suspicious, though he made it his business to check the single center-fire cinch himself for tightness before mounting. Spud was a good enough sort if you kept him away from Oakes, he thought.

Until then the claybank had been quiet, but the

moment Spud stepped back and she was free to concentrate on that unwelcome weight on her back, she went up like a Catherine Wheel on the Fourth of July, spinning crazily across the corral, sending dust flying like sparks in the sun. Lee Crosswhite hung on grimly. He took a heavy pounding in his buttocks and spine, and he could feel his neck snap hard with each jolting fall. He knew damned well she wasn't going to beat him this time, if he had to dig holes into her ribs with his knees and glue himself to the saddle with his own sweat.

The saddle gave an odd lurch. A sting of alarm chilled the back of Crosswhite's neck before he realized what was happening. The mare leaped high and twisted in air. Crosswhite felt the saddle slide with him, loose and floppy. In a world suddenly tilted awry he caught the red blur of faces, mouths gaping wide, hats waving above, and he thought, *Oakes and Spud!* Damned if they hadn't found a way to undercut that cinch. . . .

That was all the warning he had before the cinch broke and the saddle skidded sideways. Crosswhite flapped through the air like a wounded bird, pile-driving head first toward one of the corner posts of the corral.

His head missed the post or his troubles would have had a sudden end. His left shoulder slammed into unyielding wood. He careened off one of the horizontal poles in a crazy skidding fall, cracking ribs and skinning his back. Pain lit up his brain like another firecracker sizzling white and silent against a midnight sky. . . .

"Holy Infant Jesus!" someone said. "You don't think

"He's breathin'," another voice speculated. "I saw the dust stir around."

Crosswhite squeezed his eyes open a crack. Bloated faces swam out of the sun dazzle. He shut his eyes quickly against the pain. When he peered up again Oakes was bending over him. Spud gaped anxiously over his bunk buddy's shoulder.

"Crosswhite?" Oakes asked anxiously. "Can you hear me?"

Crosswhite groaned. He tried to reach for the kid's Adam's apple with both hands, but he couldn't seem to move. He thought his right hand groped feebly, but he couldn't be sure. The pain in the area of his left shoulder and in his chest was like being branded with a hot iron.

Oakes' young freckled face was wrinkled into a caricature of apprehension. "You ain't mad, are you?" he asked.

Crosswhite stared at him in amazement.

"We didn't mean nothin' personal," Oakes insisted worriedly. "It wasn't like we meant for you to get hurt bad. We was only funnin', that's all."

In spite of himself, in spite of the pain in his chest and shoulder when his body shook, Crosswhite began to laugh. He shook his head helplessly. "Damned if you don't mean it," he choked. He saw the surprise in the glance exchanged by Oakes and Spud, and he laughed until the tears ran down his cut and dust-caked face. Hesitantly at first, then with relief, the two young hands began to laugh with him.

2

"You can stay on until you mend," Frank Sells told him a few days later.

"What about that job?"

Sells shook his head. "You know better. Can't put a man out there in that high country with broken bones and only one arm to use."

"I heal fast," Crosswhite insisted.

"Not that fast, son," Sells replied. "You'll be up and around quick enough, sure, but I need a whole man out there when the snow comes. I'm sendin' Oakes and Spud."

"Oakes and Spud! Them two?"

"Yeah, I hear they pulled a prank on you with that claybank." Sells shrugged, amusement tempering his irritation over youthful highjinks. "They'll stay out of trouble up there in the high range."

"They'll more'n likely get lost," Crosswhite growled.

"They're the best I have, anyways," Sells said. "Like I told you, Crosswhite, there's no need to worry about a bunk and grub. You stay until you're fit."

"Don't need charity," Crosswhite answered stiffly. "I'll be out of your way soon as—"

"Don't talk like more of a damned fool than you are," the rancher retorted.

Crosswhite glared at him for a moment. His anger faded quickly. Sells was a hard man, but fair. And he was right, according to his lights. Cherokee, the half-breed cook who was also adept at setting bones or treating minor wounds, had concluded that Crosswhite had a badly dislocated shoulder, which he had snapped back into place, and at least two broken ribs. For the time being Crosswhite's left arm was in a sling and his chest was wrapped in a thick casing of bandage. It hurt him to take a deep breath, much less think about the duties of a solitary line rider. In offering to let him stay on until he was healed, Sells was doing as much as any rancher could. No longhorn cattleman—which was what Sells was, even though he was far from Texas and had Oregon beeves mixed with his Texans now—held onto his range or his cattle by being soft-hearted.

"I heal fast," Crosswhite repeated, but now his tone was friendlier. "But I'll take you up on stayin' on for a spell, even though that leaky bunkhouse and Cherokee's cookin' ain't much to celebrate."

"Good," Sells said gruffly. "And when you leave you might consider taking that dun mare with you, seein' as you're so partial to her. Nobody else is gonna claim her."

Lee Crosswhite grinned. His own sorrel gelding

16

was a fine cutting horse, but the durable claybank would be a valuable addition to his string, once she learned who was boss.

For some reason that made him think of Annie Macauley, far off in Cheyenne but suddenly closer, now that Crosswhite would not be wintering on the range. His grin broadened.

3

Crosswhite liked to play cards about as well as the next man, but he wasn't a reckless gambler. Ordinarily the question wouldn't even have come up, for bunkhouse gambling was forbidden to anyone who wanted to hold his job on the Rocking-S from spring through fall. When the slow season came and time was heavy, Sells eased up on this strict rule, and there was a game going almost continuously in the bunkhouse.

If he hadn't grown increasingly restless and irritable waiting for his shoulder to mend and the sling to be discarded, Crosswhite wouldn't have jumped in so deep. But there was no work and little around the ranch even to keep him busy. Almost every day he went down to the corral and talked to the dun-colored mare, and after the first week he started walking her around once more, but that activity was the high point of his day. It wasn't enough to keep a man from becoming fretful.

Besides, his terminal wages would only barely skin him through the winter, maybe not even that if he wanted to get Annie Macauley a little present to pleasure her. And with just a little piece of luck . . .

The fact that he was playing with Sut Rossiter's cards didn't bother Crosswhite in the beginning. Rossiter was one of those hands with the itchy fingers of a confirmed gambler, but Crosswhite had never heard anything spoken against his honesty. Most men would admittedly have been careful about speaking against Rossiter. His hands, with their long and nimble fingers, were good for more than deftly shuffling cards. He wore a pair of fancy ivory-handled Colts, mounted for crossdrawing, and it was rumored that his reason for hiring on at the Rocking-S that summer was a scrape down in Kansas in which a badman with a reputation as a fast gunslinger had died abruptly. There was some speculation that he was not the first man Sut Rossiter's fancy guns had dispatched to a premature accounting with his Maker.

Crosswhite expected that his luck would change—he was a thoughtful, cool-headed poker player who generally won more than he lost— even when his small losses began to mount up. But by the end of a week of playing he counted tally and discovered that he had watched nearly half of his winter stake disappear across the bunkhouse table, most of it into Rossiter's pockets.

Troubled, he began to play more recklessly, the way a man will, plunging in a manner he recognized as foolish. A man who was starting

19

to worry over his stake was the worst kind of gambler. But Crosswhite also began to pay closer attention to Sut Rossiter's hands and to the cards they dealt.

A big, solid man, handsome except for the deeply pockmarked cheeks only partially screened by flowing black handlebars, Rossiter smiled a lot as he played cards, displaying an impressive set of white, unbroken teeth. He also talked a lot, taunting and needling the other men grouped around the table with the good humor of a winner. Crosswhite knew that this was a way of distracting a man's attention from his own cards, but after a while he began to wonder if it might not also keep others from watching those long, tapering fingers closely. Rossiter won a little too steadily, taking the big pots with a regularity that was hardly credible. . . .

Rossiter wasn't really a cowhand, Crosswhite thought. He remembered that Rossiter had had to borrow working clothes, trading off one of his elegant black coats. He didn't fall out of the saddle, but he looked much more at home this way, sitting back at ease with cards in his hand and his cold gray eyes hooded like a turtle's. Crosswhite wondered if the dead gunman down in Kansas had had a quarrel with Rossiter over cards.

For two afternoons and one night of steady poker Lee Crosswhite watched patiently. Rossiter didn't make a slip. Either that, Crosswhite thought grudgingly, or he was dealing straight. But the slow erosion of Crosswhite's terminal wages continued, and Sut Rossiter, smiling and talking, continued to win.

That last night saw more of the same. By this time Crosswhite was able to move about without pain, and to breathe without driving spikes into his chest, though his left arm was still in a sling. But he was angry with himself for dissipating his wages like a wet-nosed kid coming off his first drive. He would swallow his losses if they were fairly taken. All he wanted to be certain of was that he and the other hands—for there was other muttering in the bunkhouse about Rossiter's run of luck—weren't being cheated.

Oakes and Spud still hung around the bunk-house, though they would be leaving shortly for the northern range. Oakes sat in the games most of the time, losing even more heavily than Crosswhite. His partner, Spud, was said to be on close acquaintance with every last dollar he'd ever earned.

"I'm thinkin' you oughta pull out of that game," Spud had said that morning. Hastily he added, "I told Oakes the same, Lee. I don't mean to—"

"You sayin' there's something irregular?" Crosswhite asked.

"Ain't sayin' nothin' at all," Spud insisted. "When a man's luck is runnin' against him, maybe he shouldn't oughta push it, that's all I mean."

"My troubles hasn't been all a matter of luck," Crosswhite said drily, wincing as he dried his face at the trough with his good hand. The stubble of his beard was perceptibly longer. A lot of things a man thought he did with one hand turned out to require two, like shaving.

"We're right sorry about that accident of yours," Spud said lamely. "If there was any way—"

"There ain't," Crosswhite said. "It's done. Let it go."

"It troubles me all the same." Spud hesitated. "And I don't like to see Rossiter ridin' out of here with ten men's wages in his bags."

"We're all grown up," Crosswhite snapped, cutting off the well-meant suggestion.

Later he pondered Spud's words, wondering if the young waddy wasn't as suspicious as Crosswhite that there *was* something irregular about Rossiter's good fortune at the table. Couldn't blame the kid for being nervous about voicing his suspicions out loud. Rossiter had a way of showing up suddenly without having made a sound, a quiet way of moving for such a big man.

That afternoon in the bunkhouse Crosswhite held his own, even winning a little of his stake back. When the deal came to Rossiter in his turn Crosswhite felt an inner stillness. His expression as he watched the cards flick from Rossiter's fingers was relaxed and amiable, but there was a tautness under his skin like wires pulled tight against a pole.

"Your cards have been comin' up, Crosswhite," Rossiter said, flashing his twin rows of white. "Might be your luck's changed."

"Maybe."

"Looks to me like you're all gangin' up on me," the gambler grumbled with good humor. "Why, Oakes here, he's jittery as a Mexican bean over them cards I just dealt him. How many of them are you gonna throw away, Oakes, for these new ones I'm offering?"

"None," Oakes blurted, unable to hide the brightness in his eyes. "These'll do just fine."

"Well, now." Rossiter nodded respectfully. "This here's a man's game, and that's a man's decision. How about you, Crosswhite?"

The cards were coming off the top, Crosswhite thought. Rossiter's fingers were quicker than his tongue, but not quick enough, Crosswhite was sure, to prevent his detecting a swift slide of a card from the wrong slot or sleeve when he was looking for it. He had perceived no hesitation, no extra movements calculated to divert a watchful eye. In fact, Rossiter seemed to make a deliberate show of his hands and fingers as he dealt, the hands well clear of his sleeves, the cards clearly visible. He wore no coat.

"The thing about luck is, you never know which way she's gonna jump," Rossiter rambled on. "Reckon I'll see that dollar and bump it just a leetle. She's been givin' you the cold shoulder, and when she lifts her skirts a trifle, why, you figger that means she's changed her mind, the way a woman will, and it isn't just an ankle she's gonna show you but the whole leg. But it don't necessarily mean that at all, not with luck any more than with a woman. Maybe she's just teasin' you, like maybe she's just teasin' Oakes here with those five cards he's hangin' onto so tight. You still holdin', Oakes? Those must be mighty fine cards, else you're tryin' to make us think they are. Well, damned if I don't have to see cards like those, no matter what. Gotta find out if luck is goin' all the way with you or only teasin' you with a pretty ankle."

Oakes was looking nervous now, as if he regretted staying with his opening hand. Crosswhite and Hank Bannon had dropped out, leaving only Searls, Oakes, and Rossiter in the game.

The younger man had been sitting on two pairs. Rossiter's three fives beat him, but Charley Searls had three sevens to win the pot. Nothing irregular there, Crosswhite thought with a frown. Old Charley was the honest man that Greek with the candle was always looking for. Nevertheless, the inner stillness did not leave Crosswhite. He was more convinced than ever that Rossiter had known what cards young Oakes was holding, or close enough to risk betting against him.

Wouldn't have to be all the cards, Crosswhite thought suddenly. One or two out of five were enough to make a man's guesses come out right most of the time.

Now that he was certain what he was looking for, Crosswhite was able to confirm his suspicions after two more hands, both of which Rossiter won.

"Your luck's come back," he said.

"Why, it appears that way, don't it?" Rossiter's smile flashed through the smoke from his cigar.

"Only there's no luck to it."

"That sounds to me like a man who's lost more than he could part with," Rossiter said easily.

Crosswhite flipped a face card onto the table, a jack of spades. "I didn't know how you was doin' it until now," he said quietly. "There's a pinprick near the bottom left corner. Most men hold their cards up near the top, or in the middle. You keep feelin' the bottoms."

The bunkhouse had gone completely still. Louis Bareau, a Canadian with a fiddle, put it down slowly on his bunk, but the bow he had been repairing squeaked across the strings, loud in the ticking silence. No one else moved, unless you counted Oakes licking his lips.

"Bein' a cripple ain't gonna save your hide,"

25

Rossiter said. "Less'n you want to lick my boots."

"You're dealin' a cold deck," Crosswhite said evenly. "They're your cards, and some of 'em bear your marks."

Sut Rossiter eased slowly off the end of the bench where he had been sitting. He seemed to swell as he stood. Neither he nor Crosswhite wore a weapon inside the bunkhouse—another of Frank Sells' rules. Unless Rossiter had one hidden, Crosswhite thought. A man who played a crooked hand in one game would play it in another.

"By the time you strap on iron," Rossiter said, "I'll be ready to make you swallow those words, along with some lead to make them go down easy."

"Hold on, Rossiter!" little Charley Searls jumped in. "He's on'y got one arm."

"One's enough," Crosswhite bit out, scraping his bench back and starting to rise.

"You ain't fit," Charley insisted. "Hell, I could whip you myself, condition you're in. Anyways, Sells won't stand for no gunplay."

"Charley's right," young Oakes put in anxiously. He and Spud were still feeling guilty over that cut cinch, Crosswhite thought.

There was enough muttering in agreement throughout the bunkhouse to make Rossiter's hoods drop lower over his agate eyes. Suddenly he gave a curt nod. "No man calls me a cheat," he said, baring his teeth in a mockery of a grin that was little different from his customary smile. "But quick poison is too easy. First off . . ."

Without warning he shoved the table toward Crosswhite. It caught him hard across the legs. Crosswhite stumbled against the bench and struggled for balance, hindered by young Oakes scrambling out of the way. While he was still floundering Rossiter leaped around the table and grabbed his shoulder. He saw the blow coming, but there was no way to duck it. The hard edge of Rossiter's hand slashed down like the blade of an ax. Crosswhite felt as if his left shoulder and arm had been sheared off. The pain more than the blow drove him to his knees. His eyes watered, blinding him. He heard someone yell angrily, "That's no fair way—"

"Any man wants to take his place is welcome!"

There was no one to take up Rossiter's harsh challenge. No man on that range dared to stand up to him, Crosswhite knew, because in the end it would mean going against the big gambler's twin guns.

In any event he didn't want another man fighting his battle. All he wanted was to smash one good handful of knuckles against those big white teeth.

Shaking his head, Crosswhite struggled to rise. Sut Rossiter's knee crashed into his jaw

27

and bowed him backward. Strung out on the bunkhouse floor, Crosswhite tried to roll, a chill of warning telling him what was coming next. But Rossiter's feet were quicker. The toe of his boot dug into Crosswhite's broken ribs.

Crosswhite pulled into a ball, hugging his ribs and his pain. There was a lot of yelling in the bunkhouse, but he could make no sense of it. Maybe they were cheering now. He couldn't see Rossiter through the red curtain that enveloped him, but he could feel the gambler's boots kicking his sides, searching each time for those damaged ribs. He waited, taking another boot on the bone of his hip. Then he grabbed blindly.

His hand closed on Rossiter's boot.

The rush of joy that went through him was foolish, childish, taking no account of odds. Crosswhite jerked hard. He felt Sut Rossiter leave his feet, no longer a weight to pull against but a pole falling. Rossiter slammed against the boards, making them bounce. The breath exploded from his lungs.

Crosswhite straightened like a knife blade leaping from its handle. He sprawled across Rossiter's body. His one good fist struck toward Rossiter's mouthful of teeth, but the blow glanced off the gambler's jaw as he squirmed away. Crosswhite tried to hold him down with the weight of his body, in spite of the pain in his chest and shoulder that continued to wash through him in chilling waves. Easily Rossiter broke his hold.

Crosswhite managed to stumble to his feet once more. His left arm had slipped from its sling, but it hung helplessly at his side. His right hand pawed at Rossiter's blurred shadow as it weaved toward him, parting the red curtain. The gambler brushed aside his weakened defense and drove his fists again and again into Crosswhite's arms and sides, punishing him, deliberately avoiding the open, inviting target that was Crosswhite's face.

At last the hammering blows drove him to his knees, like a sledgehammer pounding a spike into the ground. Defenseless, no longer able to protect his chest and shoulder as both arms sagged, Crosswhite knelt in the middle of the bunkhouse like a penitent.

He didn't see the boot that smashed his nose, or feel it. Later he was told that Rossiter would have continued to kick him in the ribs if Frank Sells hadn't heard the commotion and come nosing around. Then, belatedly, some of the other hands jumped in to pull Rossiter away, several men acting in concert, lashed into action out of pity or shame—or Sells' authoritative presence.

By then it made no difference to Crosswhite.

4

Sells was angry. The tangle between Crosswhite and Rossiter was exactly the reason he had a rule against bunkhouse gambling. "That's the last time I'll let up on that rule. First deck of cards I see will be their owner's ticket off this range!" He paused, glaring. "That don't do you no good, Crosswhite."

"Reckon not." The swelling of Crosswhite's torn upper lip had gone down some, but it still felt like he was talking through a wad of cloth tucked under the lip.

"Don't know when I seen a man beat up worse." The rancher's comment held no sympathy, but he added, "No use your tryin' to get up until you're fit."

"Rossiter—"

"I sent him packing, soon as I saw what happened."

"I'll catch up to him—"

"You couldn't catch a turtle in the mud," Sells said bluntly. "Anyways, Rossiter's been gone near a week."

"A week!"

"Well, five days, if you want a close tally. You been havin' yourself a good rest." The cattleman's piercing blue eyes studied Crosswhite with an

30

expression that might have hid grudging respect. "You're a fool to tackle a man like Rossiter with one arm," he said. "But I don't like a man who deals a bottom deck any more'n you do. Maybe I'd have had the guts to do the same. Like to think so."

"He put me down," Crosswhite muttered, more to himself.

"Huh!" the rancher snorted in derision. "Condition you're in, a mewling calf could have run over you. Which is another reason for lettin' Rossiter go."

"I can't do that."

"I know you can't, not permanent. But you can wait till you get your bones stuck back together. From what Cherokee tells me, Rossiter didn't do much more than hurt you real bad. I mean there's no new bones broken, 'ceptin' that one in your nose, and that isn't the first time it's been bent a little."

"No," Crosswhite said, not really listening. He fell back onto his bunk. Five days on his back, he thought. And weariness still sat on his chest as heavy as a horse. Heavy as that dun-colored mare, he thought. . . .

"You'll be headin' for Cheyenne, I expect, when you're fit to ride," Sells said. "It's my guess Rossiter will show up there sooner or later. He won't be hidin' from you. He can't let it go what you said against him, any more than you can let

31

go what he done to you. You'll meet him there, soon enough."

"Yes," Crosswhite said, the sound coming thick through his puffed lips and swollen nose. "I'll find him."

"Reckon you will," Sells said slowly. "I kinda wish . . ."

But he did not say what his wish was, whether he hoped that meeting would not occur because he feared its outcome, or simply wished that he could be there to see it. He looked down at Crosswhite with something like regret, nodded curtly, and left the bunkhouse.

Crosswhite listened to the heavy fall of the cattleman's boots, silenced abruptly as they left the boards behind. He felt fatigue pull at him, drawing him down into a dark pool.

Cheyenne, he thought. There was someone else there, and for a moment he couldn't remember who it was. No matter. Sut Rossiter would surely come. Nothing else mattered.

5

Beside a narrow stream, safely distant from the cattle country, a small band of Indians broke camp early. The morning was cold but bright. Except for the mountains and hills immediately to the west and north, the ground was clear of the earlier snowfall. The campsite was well hidden by a stand of trees that followed and protected the shoreline of the sunken stream.

The Indians moved quickly and eagerly, the younger braves expressing high spirits. They were returning to their village after a good hunt, and each man looked forward to boasting of his successes, of the buffalo hunt and the frightened trio of Crows who had fled so hastily that no one could get close enough to the enemy to claim a coup. Not that there was any merit in the incident with the Crows for these Lakota warriors, numbering eleven, but it would bring laughter at the expense of the Crows. As for the hunt, they were bringing back the meat and skins, the horns and stomachs, the useful guts and hooves and bags of a half-dozen buffalo. The village would eat well. The old ones would praise the hunters, the women would laugh and admire them, the less successful hunters would have to swallow disappointment and join in the celebration.

In the group by the stream only one was not at that moment looking ahead to their return to the village. He was their leader, White Wolf. Thoughtfully he examined the shadowy hills to the west and the rolling terrain—as yet feature-less in the first gray light of the day—to the east and south. There was nothing yet visible to disturb him—no puff of dust, no dark speck moving against the hills or the long black line of a rise. Nor had he heard anything. He had placed his ear against the bosom of the earth, a child listening to his mother's heartbeat, but there had been no sound. The earth was as still as his own mother's breast when her spirit left it to go in search of the spirit of that greatest of warriors, his father.

White Wolf selected the tallest and sturdiest of the oaks along the stream and climbed it quickly and easily, his muscular movements denying the years that had left their paths in the seams of his face like the wriggling of snakes in the sand. At the highest limb that would support his weight he stretched out and studied the reaches of the horizon now revealed to him. For a long time he lay on the branch without stirring, only his eyes shifting to some new point. He watched the fire begin to burn along the long rim of the earth to the east. At last he climbed down.

It was the way of women to shy nervously

from imagined danger, to cry out in alarm at the fierceness of shadows.

But White Wolf, the bravest of all his tribe, whose exploits had been celebrated over a hundred victorious campfires, remained uneasy.

Now he was as anxious to be under way as any of his warriors, although his reasons were different. He had not lived through so many battles, boasted of so many triumphs, earned these many tracks across his face by ignoring his instincts, the trained instincts of one who has been both hunter and hunted. Now the campsite beside the stream, which had seemed so inviting the night before when he had not felt this strange uneasiness, now this little grove of trees in the ancient trough of the stream seemed like the many teeth of a trap about to spring shut.

Two of his braves were wrestling at the edge of the stream, splashing each other with water and laughing like children. White Wolf spoke sharply, and the merriment ceased. He was not a chief who led by bellowing like thunder, but when his voice rose even slightly above its normally quiet pitch, his followers listened.

Except for his size—he was relatively tall by the standards of his people, wide of shoulder and deep of chest—there was little in either White Wolf's appearance or his quiet manner to suggest the awe in which he was held by even the fiercest of the young Sioux warriors who scorned the surrender of other chiefs to the white man's demands, and who could not understand Sitting Bull's retreat to the north. His own fierce pride was hidden by the stoic calm of his face. Its seams cut deeply to flank a broad nose and to pull down the corners of his mouth, which was wide and flat-lipped. Rather than the haughty arrogance of which he had been charged by white leaders, his expression was one of dignity and a waiting stillness, like the unruffled surface of a very deep pool. The downward pull of his lidded eyes, his lined cheeks and his mouth reflected a genuine sadness, but this was not the sadness of despair and accepted defeat. He grieved for his dead wife and his brothers who had died not in battle but on the white man's reservations. He mourned the decimation and waste of the buffalo by the white man's scornful disregard for the land and its creatures. He was saddened by the end of the good hunt—not this brief foray he had led, but the Great Hunt, which had been the way of his people for countless generations of hunters. White Wolf, paunchy with his advancing years, still saw with undimmed vision. He knew that the hunt would end soon, not only for him but for all his people.

This did not explain his morning's unease. The pony soldiers had been active during the time of the Yellow Leaf Moon, but White Wolf had eluded them easily, keeping to the hills and bluffs. Then had come the first snows of winter. The soldiers had withdrawn. For two winters past they had marched through the deepest snows in great force, hunting the Sioux and Cheyennes, seeking vengeance for their terrible defeat on the banks of the Little Big Horn, but now their eagerness had diminished, thinned out by the spilled blood of too many victories. White Wolf had waited until his scouts brought assurances that the soldiers no longer rode far from their camps. Then he had left his village with ten young warriors to hunt the buffalo his scouts had discovered to the south. The first snows had cleared, and the gods had smiled upon the earth. It was the time of false summer, when the striped gopher emerged from his hole to have one last look at the trees and the grass and the sun before disappearing for the winter. It was a good time for the hunt.

Returning now toward his village, White Wolf knew that the fine days of the year were almost over. It was nearly the season of the Frost Moon, the days and nights of freezing cold, of snows that mantled the earth in silence, and of hunger.

Impatient now, restless as the deer sensing danger it cannot see, White Wolf started toward his horse, which was hobbled among the trees.

6

Late on the previous afternoon a detachment of cavalry, under the command of Captain Arthur A. Austin, of the Maryland Austins, had chanced across the tracks of a small band of Indians, their trail moving northwest along a ridge that overlooked a small stream. Austin had halted his men and called for Sergeant Angus Jamison, his chief scout.

The time was the last day of October. Some six weeks or so earlier two Cheyenne chiefs, Little Wolf and Dull Knife, had escaped from the Indian reservation far to the south. After a remarkable flight on stolen horses through the Indian Territory and across Kansas, the Cheyenne runaways had successfully crossed the South Platte and reached their old hunting grounds in the Niobrara Hills. Along the way they had managed to do what Austin would have thought impossible—filter through at least four of the five overlapping military barriers that stretched from the Santa Fe Trail to the Black Hills, manned by thirteen thousand soldiers.

Once in familiar terrain the two chiefs had parted company. The younger Little Wolf and his followers had disappeared to the north. Dull Knife's group, mostly old men and women, had soon been discovered by searching cavalry. On October 23 the old chief had surrendered.

Little Wolf had not been found.

In the days since Dull Knife's capture, troops of cavalry had fanned out to the north and west, searching for the trail of the elusive and dangerous Little Wolf. Austin's detachment was one of these search parties. His troops and their horses were fresh, the late October weather remained uncommonly mild, and he wondered as he waited for Jamison if he were about to be uncommonly lucky.

Jamison was more skeptical. "It's not enough tracks to be Little Wolf's party," the wiry scout said, scraping a stiff red brush that covered his chin.

"How many are there, would you say?"

"A dozen at most. Maybe less if they have any extra horses packing meat."

"Do you believe it's a hunting party, Sergeant?"

"Seems likely, sir."

"Couldn't it be a hunting party from Little Wolf's entourage?"

Sergeant Jamison blinked at the word. Captain Austin was an educated man for sure, a West Pointer and a career officer. He was also young, somewhere in his mid-twenties, or a good ten years the sergeant's junior, and ambitious. When you put these factors together they didn't always add up to happy riding for the cavalry in the

West, but Austin had surprised him more than once. He listened, for one thing; he didn't assume that his arsenal of fine words and his handsome features guaranteed either the respect of his men or the eternal rightness of his judgments.

"It could be that, sir, but more'n likely they'd be renegade Sioux."

"Why do you think that, Sergeant?"

"From what we was told at the Red Cloud Agency, Captain, this Little Wolf broke out of the Indian Territory some time in September."

"Go on."

Captain Austin was squinting at the hills to the west, as if he were not paying close attention, but Jamison knew that he was. The captain liked to look away when he was concentrating on what you said, as if a man's eyes and mouth distracted him from what he was hearing.

"Well, sir, I'm thinkin' that means he's come nearly a thousand miles in somethin' like six weeks to get this far. The way he went across Kansas, seems like he was making sixty or seventy miles a day. Cavalry couldn't keep up with him."

Captain Austin turned to look at Jamison with a faint smile, as if he appreciated a small joke on the cavalry. "So you don't think we can catch him either, is that it, Jamison?"

"No, sir, beggin' your pardon, sir, not exactly that at all. Thing is, it's been a week since Dull

Knife was caught, after him and Little Wolf split up. And we don't even know exactly when that split-up happened. So it's my guess Little Wolf could be clear up in Montana Territory by now, the way he was travelin'. Wouldn't be no reason for him to stop."

Austin nodded thoughtfully, peering again at the ragged outline of the western hills. Relieved of the old and sick who had surrendered with Dull Knife, the hot young bloods who had stayed with Little Wolf would have been able to move even faster. They really were quite remarkable horsemen, the captain reflected. And he would like nothing better than to take up the chase, no matter how far north it led. His men were well outfitted for this winter campaign, clothed in woolens, some of them carrying the coveted furs. While these had not been needed in late October, during the brief span of belated summerlike weather, those conditions could change rapidly. They were up to it, Austin thought, and he would relish the chase—but his orders prohibited such a lengthy pursuit, not to mention his supplies. Even to contemplate it was, if not unsoldierly, at best amateurish.

A small hunting party, barely an hour or two ahead of the detachment, was something else entirely.

"That sounds reasonable, Sergeant Jamison," Austin said with approval. "We'll take it that this is a small party of Sioux mavericks, or a hunting party from a larger group, or, on a very long chance, some of Little Wolf's followers. In any event, it seems that we ought to find out, doesn't it?"

"Yes, sir. Could even be—" Jamison fell silent.

"Out with it, Sergeant. If you have any other ideas, let's hear them."

Jamison grinned. Damned if Austin wasn't a different breed of West Point officer. "Could be some of White Wolf's people," he said. "He's still on the loose."

White Wolf! Captain Arthur Austin could not deny the sharp thrill that made him stiffen, sitting even more erectly in the saddle. Little Wolf was a renowned and certainly remarkable warrior, but even at West Point Austin had listened to lectures about the older White Wolf and the other great Indian warleaders of the plains. White Wolf had fought at the Rosebud. He was among that confederacy of Sioux and Cheyennes who had surprised Custer at Little Big Horn. He had sat in council with Sitting Bull and Crazy Horse as an equal. He had been a scourge of the U. S. Cavalry in the West for a dozen years, and a great Sioux chief for as many years before that. Stubborn, recalcitrant, and proud—he was all of these things. And a brilliant tactician. The few times he had deigned to attend peace conferences with the whites he had infuriated the white generals he had faced by attitudes they classified as arrogant and insufferable—not that the generals couldn't get their backs up easily, or show arrogance themselves on occasion, Austin thought. White Wolf had simply acted as if the whites were intruders. All they had to do to end hostilities, he had said, was to withdraw from Sioux hunting lands. His terms were outrageously simple, and he was not amenable to any sort of bargaining over them.

With Crazy Horse dead, murdered at the Red Cloud Agency over a year ago, and with Sitting Bull in exile in Canada, where he had retreated to safety, most of the Sioux had come wearily into the reservation, the fight gone out of them. A few maverick bands held out, harassing forts and trails, carrying on the hopeless fight. White Wolf was one of these—perhaps the most honored of the Sioux warleaders still in the field.

"That's all I needed to hear, Sergeant," the captain said with a grin. "We'll see where these tracks take us. And send me those two Shoshone scouts of yours; I'd like a word with them. Maybe it takes an Indian to catch another Indian without being obtrusive."

Sergeant Angus Jamison grinned in response as he wheeled away. Obtrusive, he thought. Obtrusive!

• • •

Austin's Shoshone scouts discovered the Indian camp in the first hour of full darkness. They verified Jamison's guess that the Indians were a Sioux hunting party, laden with buffalo, and that there were no more than ten or eleven warriors in the group—a third of the number of men under Austin's command. There were neither women nor children, Austin heard with satisfaction; the hunters must be en route to their village. In the heat of battle, troops could not always be told to verify their targets before shooting, and Austin had no wish to join that ample company of U. S. Cavalry officers in the Army of the West whose fame had been erected on the bodies of infants and women and enfeebled old men.

The young captain discussed the terrain with the Indian scouts and with Jamison. The sergeant respectfully suggested that a move might be made at once, while they could creep up on the Indians under cover of darkness, since it would be virtually impossible to approach closely in daylight without being detected. Attacked in the open and on horseback, the Indians would have a much better chance to escape. The argument was a sound one, the logical maneuver. But if Austin's adversary were White Wolf himself, might he not anticipate exactly such a move?

Austin retreated to his tent to ponder his

decision. Jamison was an old hand at fighting Indians, but there were strong arguments against his plan. Certainly darkness would cover their approach, but once the first surprise of the attack was over that darkness would work to the advantage of the Indians. Austin did not have enough men to make an attack in force along the river bottom and at the same time to close off the two flanks of the Indian camp on either side of the river. In the dark many would escape either upstream or through gaps in Austin's lines. The cavalry's fire would have to be tempered by the knowledge that shadowy figures in the darkness could be either friend or foe.

Moreover, the heavy concentration of trees along the bottom, where the Sioux had camped, would also offer ample protection after the first volley. Even if they were pinned down among those trees, the enemy would be enabled to hold out for some time under good cover, inflicting severe casualties—a price Austin was not willing to pay.

He was, as Jamison had broadly hinted to the officer, an unusual West Pointer.

He had to drive the Indians out of that position, Austin reasoned. To the north the trees thinned out. The stream swung to the northwest about a half mile up, and its western flank fell away into a broad and open valley, overlooked by a higher promontory of rocky ground that formed the east bank of the cut. If he had ten men with rifles on that rocky bluff, Austin thought . . .

At midnight he called both Sergeant Jamison and Lieutenant Ernest Schaefer, a shavetail close to Austin's age anticipating his first direct skirmish with the hostiles, into his tent. Before dawn, he explained, Schaefer would take ten men in a wide swing to the north, returning to the stream at a point well above the Indian encampment, and proceeding at the last on foot. There Schaefer would deploy his men under as good cover as he could find on the bluffs overlooking the stream bed. The rest of the detachment would approach the camp from the south, timing their arrival at first light—but only on word from advance scouts that the Indians had decamped and were on the move.

"Their tracks lead north," Austin said. "There's good reason to believe they'll move out in the same direction. Once they're clear of that heavy cover we'll give them reason to keep going."

"We're not gonna hit anything, chargin' up their tails," Jamison growled. But the respect in his squinting appraisal of the young officer had, if anything, deepened.

Austin smiled. "That will be Lieutenant Schaefer's assignment."

7

The first rifle shot cracked from a point south of the Indian camp just as they were leaving it. Its report was as brittle as the snap of a dry branch in the cool air of that November morning, the first day of the Frost Moon. Directly in front of White Wolf a young brave looked up at the sky in surprise, made a small gurgling sound in his throat and, as his pony jumped nervously ahead, slid sideways from his mount to pitch onto his face among red and yellow leaves. On the dying echo of that first shot a noisy and furious charge came from the Indians' rear.

In the pandemonium of that surprise attack, White Wolf saw many things. He understood that he had not listened attentively enough to the whispering of his hunter's instinct. He realized that the blue-coated pony soldiers, many of them wearing the skins of bears, outnumbered his band many times. He saw that they were attacking along the bed of the stream as well as along the higher ground on both banks, but the main attack was along the bottom.

And he knew that something was wrong. The attack, though carried out with surprise, was both too late and too early. Too late, for it had failed to catch the Indians sleeping or only beginning to stir at the approach of dawn. And too early, because the whooping of the soldiers and the random rifle fire and the shrill trumpeting of a bugle had warned the Indians, spurring them into flight before many had been struck down. The bullet that had killed the warrior so close to White Wolf had been a lucky chance, fired from some distance. . . .

No! Alarm struck White Wolf like the stabbing of an enemy knife. That one shot had not been a wild chance from horseback or from the riverbank. It had come from above—from a lone sniper in a tree. And the cavalry attack was more like an Indian raid than a typical maneuver of the pony soldiers. White Wolf's band was already racing along the bottomland in panicky flight— exactly what the white chief had designed! The noise, the bugle, the premature shooting—all deliberate, part of a plan.

"No! Wait!" he shouted. "Do not run—it is a trick!"

But his cry was scattered by the wind. His braves were already racing out of his control. The best cover of the trees was already behind them. They were still contained by the shallow flanks of the stream, but shortly ahead, as White Wolf and many of the others remembered, there was the open plain. No Indian believed that he could be caught in the open astride his favorite pony.

The white chief had counted on that, too, White Wolf thought bitterly.

Anger boiled in his throat. He hung low over the neck of his pony, trying to drive it by the force of his will to overtake his fleeing band. "Stop!" he commanded. "Turn back—this is not a good way to die!"

His wind-caught urging came too late. The first fleeing warriors swept toward the opening that appeared on the left bank of the stream where the broad plain beckoned. Just as they reached that opening a wall of flame crackled from the high ground above the east bank. Two horses buckled simultaneously, ponies and riders plunging into a turmoil of dust and flying limbs. Another warrior threw his arms high and screamed, as if he were going into battle instead of leaving it. The white chief had planned well, White Wolf thought. His riflemen were shooting the ponies.

A warrior's rage seized him. He could no longer hope to stop the others. He had been outwitted, his braves routed. But if this was the end of the hunt, he would not succumb like the soft-eyed deer in frightened flight but like the snarling wolf backed into a crevice, the wolf for which he had been named in that long-lost golden time of his birth.

White Wolf wheeled his pony in a skilled and astonishingly quick maneuver. Almost in the instant of decision he had turned about and was racing back along his own tracks—straight into the fury of the cavalry's pursuit.

Their charge had closed the gap on the fleeing Indians, and in flashing seconds White Wolf was among them. Horses and men reared and plunged around him. Though he held his rifle in one hand, he made no effort to shoot. Instead, seeing a slender figure with a sword brandished high in his right hand, White Wolf swung toward him. Whirling past the officer—for who else but the white chief raised a long knife instead of a rifle?—White Wolf reached out and touched him.

Then, as suddenly as he had swung about, he was through the lines of the bluecoats—a thinner and more ragged line than he had first guessed, for there were as many soldiers on the two flanks of the stream as there were in the cut. White Wolf plunged past them. He broke clear, racing along the bottom while the noise of battle swiftly faded away. For the first time since the opening rifle shot of the brief battle, White Wolf saw that he could live to hunt again. He had lost the battle, but he had counted coup on the white chief who had defeated him, even though there was no Indian witness to give that coup the merit it deserved. He could now escape with honor.

He did not hear the shot that struck him. It was lost in the sounds of many shots. He felt the blow on his back, low and to the left. The impact knocked him forward over his pony's neck. He nearly lost his balance and fell off, but his left leg managed to hook securely under the rope that went under the pony's belly. After a precarious moment White Wolf was able to struggle into position on the pony's back once more. He hunched forward in pain, clinging to the pony's mane with his right hand. His rifle was gone. He could not remember dropping it when the bullet struck.

There would be no bragging of this wound. It would bring him no honor. Was it to be his fate to die with a wound in his back, the wound of the fleeing deer instead of the wolf?

8

Astonished by the Indian warrior's bold maneuver, Captain Arthur Austin, like all of his men, had been too slow to cut the hostile down when he whirled about and plunged directly into their lines. Austin had seen the black eyes fix suddenly upon him as the warrior changed his racing pony's course. In that moment the young officer had felt the first bowel-deep fear he had known in his life, a chilling consciousness of death descending upon him with a swiftness and certainty he could not alter or evade.

Instead of the crushing blow there had been only fingers clutching briefly at his arm—that was all. There was a nightmare vision of braided hair and dark skin and a few feathers bobbing in the wind. Then the Indian was gone.

Plunging on, the chill of panic still gripping his neck and his bowels, Austin had reached the open plain before he was able to rein in his speeding horse. By then the battle, such as it was, was almost over. A half-dozen Indians and at least as many horses lay sprawled in grotesque positions along the river bottom and the widening valley. Puffs of dust and dark specks within them showed a few survivors in flight across the plain, the cavalry in hot pursuit. Lieutenant

Schaefer was standing on the bluff overlooking the stream, waving his rifle over his head and shouting in exultation, his face red with triumph, as if it had caught the glory of the sun, which was rising behind him. Triumph, Austin thought, and relief with himself for carrying out his part in that small victory. He had been through his first battle. Looking around at the crumpled postures of death, he felt no such pleasure now.

Sergeant Jamison raced up to him. He reined his black horse to a skidding stop. His red beard bristled, and his eyes shone with excitement. "It was him, Captain!" Jamison shouted. "It was him!"

"Him?" Austin repeated stupidly. "Who do you—"

"The one who counted coup on you, sir. That's him, I'm sure as I am of the devil. You been touched by White Wolf himself!"

9

White Wolf could feel the blood of life seeping out of him, as if his very spirit drained away in liquid drops that vanished upon the matted plain, there to be trampled by the heedless buffalo of future suns whose warmth he would not feel upon his back.

Sometimes now the sun turned dark as he rode. He was heading southwest toward the nearest hills that might offer refuge. Far behind him came the small clotted figures of the pony soldiers in dogged chase. How many? White Wolf could not trust his eyes—those black eyes that had rivaled the eagle's. His vision wavered, blurred. A dozen bluecoats perhaps. Their number did not matter.

His arms, whose corded slenderness did not suggest their bowman's strength, were now as weak as a woman's. He clung to his pony's back more by instinctive balance than by the waning strength of arms and legs.

Had the white leader joined in the chase? White Wolf had decided that it was no shame to be bested by such a formidable warrior, a young fighter seemingly as beardless as an Indian. But he would like to survive to meet this enemy in another battle.

The hills loomed close, a humpbacked southerly range of the Black Hills, notched by deep canyons. White Wolf knew these hills well, as he knew all the hills and canyons, all the valleys and rivers of these ancient hunting grounds of his people. There were cliffs where no white man could ever follow him. But would his woman's arms enable him to climb walls he had easily scaled in the past?

How many of his warriors had fallen this morning because of their leader's failure? This too was a heavy burden for him to carry when he had left so much of his strength and his spirit scattered behind him across the plain. And what would become of *their* spirits, those dead whose bodies were not reclaimed from the vengeance of the white soldiers?

He rode among low foothills, deliberately letting his pursuers see him. The thin report of a rifle shot reached him belatedly, the sound carrying where no bullet could fly. White Wolf nodded, his head heavy upon his neck, and dipped out of sight.

The canyon he had chosen lay straight ahead. His tracks led toward it. At the last moment he veered south over rocky ground.

A half mile farther on, at the foot of an ancient animal trail almost hidden behind brush at the mouth of another canyon, White Wolf regretfully abandoned his pony. "Do not be sad, little one," he said. "Run free. Run like the wind, and remember who rode with you."

He knew in his heart that they would no longer ride together.

The steep and narrow animal trail climbed the canyon wall where it seemed impassable. At the top a pass led over the bluffs. There he would rest.

From somewhere within he found the strength to begin that tortuous climb. Always he listened for the sounds of pursuit. At one point a blackness came like the velvet sweetness of a summer night in his tipi. He woke from it suddenly, startled and afraid, as if he were a child.

He heard them then, searching.

Halfway up that steep and broken face he felt the last remaining strength begin to drain away, like water from a broken bowl. Then he came to a small ledge where a scrub pine clung amidst clumps of stubborn grass. Facing the ledge was a narrow fissure, wedge-shaped, formed by two huge leaning slabs of granite. Across the ledge were the scattered remnants of a nest. The eagle had been born here, White Wolf thought. Here he had eaten and tested his wings. Here he had taken flight.

From this perch, if he must die, his own spirit could soar above the earth he had loved, above the dark trees and the mountains, above the hunting grounds and the cool streams.

Then, looking closer, White Wolf discovered other debris, not the eagle's but man's. At the bottom of the fissure was a natural pit hollowed out by the hunter's tools into a trough in which a man could lie upon his back. In the pit were many of the wooden poles that had once been placed across the pit as beams, remnants of rawhide rope, clumps of sod, now taking fresh root, which had perhaps been used to cover the trap. Here the hunter had waited for the eagle to soar high above him, to circle and wheel and glide over the ledge until the great bird decided there was no danger. Here, through the opening in his hidden trap, the hunter's arms had reached out to seize the eagle's legs and drag him, flapping and screaming, into the pit.

Wounded and weak and sick, White Wolf still smiled in memory of the unknown hunter. Then, armed only with his knife and his courage, he lay in the pit, half-hidden beneath the leaning rocks.

If the enemy discovered him here, he thought, they would find him as dangerous as the eagle had found the unknown hunter.

10

Lee Crosswhite had circled north rather than heading directly toward Cheyenne. He rode through an area of small cattle ranches set between two minor mountain ranges. It was pretty country, Crosswhite thought, green and well-watered. It wasn't many years ago that the cattlemen down in Texas were taking wagers on how long any rancher would last up in these high plains, where no cattle could possibly survive the terrible winters. But already events were proving them wrong. Wishbone Hines had seen the light early, investing everything he had in a section of land and a small herd. Crosswhite had helped his old saddle partner drive those beeves north. Wishbone would have liked him to stay on, but Crosswhite didn't think either of them was ready for that just yet.

"I'll need a good man to strawboss this outfit," Wishbone had said.

"Time you got anythin' to boss, maybe I'll be ready to settle down," Crosswhite had replied. But he didn't believe it, then or now. He didn't know how he would take to being tied to one place. He'd been moving as long as he could remember, first with his pa and ma from Ohio to Missouri and from there to Colorado. And in the dozen years since the war on his own, across Texas and all the way to California and back, working his way wherever hc went. He had scouted and hunted game for a wagon train, earned mail, ridden shotgun on a stagecoach, and eventually drifted into cowpunching down in the Panhandle. He liked that about as well as anything he'd tried—the men and the work, the long drives as much as the spring and fall branding, the feeling of being free and loose and part of the land, always knowing that he could move on when he was ready.

He half-regretted the swing north to visit Wishbone Hines, but the bowlegged little rancher would be disappointed if Crosswhite rode within fifty miles and failed to stop by.

"Any time yo' come this way, you've always got a roof to keep yo' dry and a meal to fill yo' belly," Wishbone had insisted. "I'd take it as real unfriendly if'n yo' wasn't to think o' my place like it was yo' own."

It was late afternoon when Crosswhite recognized the landmarks Hines had once pointed out to him—a lone cedar growing out of a steeple of rocks, a notch in one of the hills behind the steeple, a shallow stream with a rocky bed that slanted out of the hills across a green valley. He was glad enough to be nearly "home," even though it wasn't his own. The long ride from the Rocking-S had been uneventful, but he carried more aches than he could remember riding with for many a year. The left shoulder bothered him especially, although he had discarded his arm sling. After a day in the saddle it seemed as if he could feel every step the sorrel took jarring straight through to his collarbone.

The big claybank mare trailed behind on a lead. She wasn't ready to let a man ride her yet, but she had proved docile enough on the trail, willing to follow the sorrel and finally amenable to carrying a light pack. "You'll have your time," Crosswhite kept telling her each day. He was learning patience.

Patience, and reluctant acceptance of Frank Sells' good advice, was one reason Crosswhite had decided to accept Wishbone Hines' invitation. He was not quite ready to meet Sut Rossiter in Cheyenne. He had to be whole for that encounter when it came. His left shoulder ached, and sometimes his ribs complained, but the bones were knitting, the bruised flesh already healed. Those cracked bones felt the cold more, especially the last night or so, as if heralding an ominous change in the weather, already overdue. But a few more days of rest at Hines' place would put him in shape to tackle a bear.

Or Sut Rossiter.

It had been over a year since Crosswhite last saw the Wishbone brand on a cow or the thin trail of smoke climbing over Hines' small shack. Now he saw that same thread of smoke rising, and he grinned as he urged the sorrel into a trot. Topping a rise, he was surprised to see that Hines' shack had grown an extra room at one end, along with a storage shed near the corral and another building that might have been a small bunkhouse or chicken coop—"Use it either way," Crosswhite could hear Hines saying. He rode in eagerly, suddenly glad he had come.

He had almost reached the small cluster of buildings before he noticed something that made him pull up abruptly. Behind the elongated shack, spread out on some bushes to dry, were some clothes that wouldn't have looked right on Wishbone Hines or any other man. Specifically, an assortment of ruffled petticoats and dresses.

"Lee! Lee Crosswhite, or I'm seein' ghosts!" Hines burst through the door of the shack and ran toward him, his short bandy legs churning up less dust on that hard ground than their activity warranted. "If'n yo' ain't a sight fo' sore eyes!"

"Howdy, Wishbone." But Crosswhite was gaping past his old friend toward the doorway he had vacated. Standing in it was a young girl whose ripe figure strained at her cotton dress like a grape about to burst.

"Yo' is jest in time fo' supper." Wishbone grinned up at him. "Climb down and feed yo' tapeworm."

"It's been goin' hungry. But—"

"Don't have to say it. No need to tell yo' ol' Wishbone ain't takin' to wearin' petticoats. No, sir, they ain't mine, Lee—they belongs to Mama."

"Mama?" Crosswhite repeated in disbelief. He was trying not to stare too hard at the girl in the doorway. The lamplight inside the shack threw her uninhibited ripeness into bold relief in the gathering dusk. "You mean you, uh, got yourself hitched, Wishbone?"

"Don't blame yo' fo' lookin' like yo' swallowed a bee," Hines said with a gleeful cackle. "Wouldn't o' believed it myself if'n anybody had tol' me as much a year ago. Here, the boy can water yo' hosses. Yo' jest come right on into the house. Jimmy! Here, boy, yo' take good care of Mr. Crosswhite's hosses."

A gawky youth of fourteen or fifteen appeared from nowhere, ducked his head in acknowledgment of Crosswhite's greeting, and led the sorrel and the claybank away. Then Crosswhite followed Wishbone Hines toward the shack, still not quite able to believe what he was seeing and hearing.

Wishbone Hines was a bantam rooster of a man, feisty and hot-tempered—all quick, as another rider had once said, carefully out of Wishbone's hearing. But underneath that surface belligerence was a heart that was all sentiment and loyalty, Crosswhite knew. Wishbone was as readily moved to tears or laughter as he was to anger. And he was one whose fidelity to a friend would never bend an inch. The truth was that he wasn't much to look at, Crosswhite thought. He was scrawny and bowlegged, ten years older than Crosswhite, and with neck seams for every year. The notion that he had married the girl who had now disappeared into the shack was not easily swallowed. But how did that account for Jimmy?

"Cynthia!" Wishbone called ahead happily. "Wait'll yo' meet my little woman, Crosswhite. And wait'll yo' light into some of her chuck. Yo' ain't never tasted nothin' like it out of no wagon, son. She jest fed me one little ol' meal and I was hooked!"

She was hardly old enough to know how to cook beans, Crosswhite thought. Then, as they stepped into the shack, he had his second surprise.

"Mama, this here's Lee Crosswhite, that yo' have heard me tell of so many times yo' musta been sick o' listenin'." Wishbone beamed happily. "An' this here's my Cynthia."

Crosswhite mumbled something, feeling his cheeks and his neck redden with embarrassment. Wishbone Hines' Cynthia turned out to be a hearty, handsome woman, buxom and round, as ample and imposing physically as Wishbone was small. There was a smell of flour about her, like the smell of a flour sack, and a warm, ruddy glow in her full cheeks. Her hair was streaked with gray.

Crosswhite's embarrassment did not lessen when Hines turned to the young girl standing beside the table with a stack of white china plates in her hands, staring at Crosswhite with her full lower lip caught between small white teeth.

"This here's little Leota," the bandy-legged rancher said with obvious pride. "Leota Hines now, and that's the fact of it, if'n she wants to call herself so. Ain't that right, little 'un?"

The girl giggled. That dress is going to come right apart, Crosswhite thought with awe.

"An' yo' met Jimmy outside. Jimmy and Leota is Mama's two young'uns, what she had with her first, who passed away on the trail west. Why, I got me a made-to-order little family, Lee. All in one swoop!"

The girl was fifteen, it turned out—younger than she appeared. And the boy was also younger than Crosswhite had guessed, his gawky height making him look more than his thirteen years.

"You're right welcome to sit down with us, Mr. Crosswhite," Cynthia Hines said, but there was a speculative sharpness in her blue eyes that tempered the welcome.

It was too much for Crosswhite to take in all at once. He felt clumsy and uncomfortable with his old friend. He wasn't sure what he said or how he got through the meal that followed. Wishbone hardly stopped talking, telling his widow woman and his adopted youngsters how he had ridden the long trail from Texas to Ogallala with Crosswhite, exaggerating tales of mavericks and desperados and dangers they had met and conquered together. Cynthia Hines seemed appreciative of the praise of her cooking prodded out of Crosswhite by Wishbone's enthusiasm. It was plain fare, but good and plentiful. During the meal she was neither hostile nor overly friendly, but Wishbone seemed not to notice, his happiness at the meeting making up for any lack.

She had once looked like her daughter, Crosswhite thought. There was something almost comical about the way a woman of her present size could dote on a little man like Wishbone as she did. She's willing to accept me because of him, he thought. But what is it that's worrying her?

"Here, Leota, pass along another piece of apple pie to ol' Lee. Ain't that the best yo' ever put a tooth to, Crosswhite?"

"Surely is." He tried not to stare at the girl's breathtaking bosom straining against her dress as she reached past him. She giggled when Crosswhite coughed. She giggled a lot, he noticed.

It was about then that Cynthia Hines began to question him about his work and what brought him this far north and where he was going.

"Got throwed by a horse," Crosswhite said,

accounting for any visible marks remaining from his fight with Sut Rossiter in the bunkhouse. "Stove in a couple ribs and this here shoulder, and done myself out of a winter place."

"Well, don't yo' look no further," Wishbone Hines said. "Yo' knows that yo' kin stay here long as yo' likes. Why, they's room to rattle in the bunkhouse I been buildin'. I'll be needin' hands come spring fo' roundin' up, so I figgered I'd need a roof for 'em. There's plenty to do, Lee—more'n me and the boy kin handle."

"I expect Mr. Crosswhite has plans of his own, Papa," Cynthia Hines said.

Crosswhite eased back from the table, feeling as stuffed inside his jeans after that second piece of pie as little Leota looked in her dress. "Yes, ma'am," he said. "I'm headin' for Cheyenne."

"Yo' ain't doin' nothin' o' the kind!" Wishbone Hines protested. "Why, yo' jest got off yo' hoss, Lee. Surely yo' mean to stay a spell."

"I have to meet someone in Cheyenne."

"Well, dammit, he can wait, cain't he? Yo's welcome here as long as yo' wants to stay."

Cynthia Hines said nothing. Although she seemed busy at that moment clearing the table, her silence made Crosswhite wonder just how welcome he was. It would have been different if Wishbone had been alone, as he had expected. But what did Wishbone's Cynthia have against him? Was it only that he was someone from

Wishbone's past—a past that he might long for and she wanted him to forget? It didn't seem to Crosswhite that she had anything to worry about in that way.

It was a quiet evening. Wishbone showed Crosswhite around his place—what they could see in the darkness as the long night of early winter closed down quickly. "We can ride out tomorrow and look over the herd," the rancher said proudly. He went away to find a kerosene lantern to show his old partner the work he had been doing on the new bunkhouse. "She's tight enough, Lee," he pointed out. "Ain't got no bunks in yet, but—"

"She'll do fine, Wishbone."

He was ready to turn in then, weary from days of riding, but Wishbone insisted they have a last smoke together, sitting on the step off the porch that fronted the main shack. Calling it a shack was no longer fair to it, Crosswhite thought. It was turning into a real home. He wondered if what he felt for Wishbone then was a kind of envy. Wishbone sure seemed happy enough. He had that boy grinning all the time and running to do his chores, and Cynthia mothering him in a possessive way. And that little Leota . . .

Time came when any man would have to think of settling down. Maybe there was something to be said for having solid walls and a tight roof you chinked up yourself, for not having to scratch all the time to survive, for trading the haphazard partnerships of the saddle for the close, warm loving Wishbone had found.

This was what Annie had always been hinting around at, Crosswhite mused. Annie Macauley, who was waiting for him there in Cheyenne, like Sut Rossiter. Well, not waiting for him exactly, but always glad to see him when he came.

"Yo' should settle down," Wishbone said, as if reading Crosswhite's thoughts. "Find yo'self a good woman. Hell, there's good land hereabouts that's still goin' begging. Man's got to start thinkin' about the time when he's too old to be gettin' hisself throwed by an onery hoss."

"Yeah." Why was it, Crosswhite speculated, that a man always felt compelled to sell others on the course he had chosen for himself?

"Yo' think about it, Lee."

"I'll do that."

He hadn't told Wishbone Hines about Sut Rossiter. And he couldn't point out that there was no sense in his making any plans at all beyond Cheyenne.

When Wishbone at last withdrew into the warmth of the house and his family, and Crosswhite trudged down toward the corral to check on the sorrel and the claybank before bedding down for the night, he felt an unaccustomed loneliness, a sense of being left out in the cold. The night sky was partly cloudy. Here and there a star showed through, distant and cold, as lonely in its isolation as a man could be in this vast prairie when he passed by a house or a shack where yellow light stained the windows and merry voices sounded.

Hell, that's only one side of it, he growled to himself. There's light and company in many a jail cell, too.

He stamped back to the bunkhouse. In the darkness he did not see Leota Hines until he heard a soft rustle that made him peer sharply at the doorway. "Pa says you might want this." She pressed a small earthenware jug into Crosswhite's hands. Whisky sloshed in the jug. "It gets cold in this shack."

She giggled, and Crosswhite could feel his cheeks warming in the darkness. He remembered how her body jiggled whenever she laughed like that.

Suddenly the girl was standing very close to him. He could smell her, a scent of hair and dough and cotton and soft flesh. He swallowed and his chest felt heavy and he could feel himself leaning back. Lord, didn't she know enough to guess how it was with a man when he's been three or four months without ever seeing a town or a woman?

"I'm glad you came, Mr. Crosswhite," she said in a rush. "I hope you mean to stay with us for a *good* long spell. You *do* mean to stay, don't you?"

"Well, uh—"

"I'm glad." She wasn't giggling now, and she didn't even sound much like a child whispering in the darkness. "Ain't nothin' *ever* happens out here—nothin' exciting. You can't imagine how lonely it can be."

"Uh, yes, I can see how that would be."

"I gotta go. Mama will be wonderin' about me. Oh, I *am* glad you came, Mr. Crosswhite!"

She hugged him impulsively, the way a child will. Crosswhite stood rooted long after she had slipped away and disappeared in the darkness. He hadn't even cared about the way his ribs hurt when she hugged him. He could still feel the melting softness of her, as if she had left an imprint along the whole lean, hard length of his body.

He stared toward the house. *That's why,* he thought suddenly. That's why Wishbone's woman wasn't being friendly. That's why she's afraid of having you hang around.

Hearing their voices sometime during the night, he stepped outside the bunkhouse. He hadn't slept very soundly, and the voices had been raised for some time. They carried to him clearly under the cold stars, more of which were visible now.

"Yo' cain't ask me to turn him out. A man jest don't turn a friend out."

"He's a drifter. I won't have . . ."

The answer died away, then rose again.

". . . she's just a child. She's not answerable."

"Well, yo' don't have to worry none about Lee, Mama. Hell's fire, woman—"

"It isn't him I'm worrying about."

No, Crosswhite thought. It wasn't him she had to worry about. He grinned suddenly. That girl was going to cause a whole lot of worrying before she was ripe enough to fall off the tree.

"Yo' cain't ask me that," Wishbone said with a note of desperation in his voice.

"She's your daughter now, Papa, same as she's mine. You have to think of that. And I won't have her gettin' into any trouble with every hangdog rider that comes along. Why, he's about as much use for a girl to set her heart on as a tumbleweed."

"Cynthia, yo' ain't bein' fair. I tell yo' . . ."

The argument went on for a long time after Crosswhite stopped listening. Long before it ended he knew what he had to do.

Crosswhite left in the morning. Wishbone protested, but he had used up all his arguments during the night. Crosswhite thanked Cynthia Hines for her hospitality—and immediately felt guilty about making her look guilty. He left hastily. Departing the valley, he kept remembering the way little Leota had stared at him as he sat his sorrel and said goodbye, her lower lip thrust out in a pout.

11

The *wasicu* did not see him. White Wolf crouched motionless in the brush with a stoic patience that paid no heed to the deep wound in his back, to his weakness, to his hunger.

Wasicu. The white man. The enemy. White Wolf could smell him, just as he could smell the meat that the man had seared over his small fire and eaten. The light, soft snow that had fallen through the evening and into the night had smothered the familiar smells of the earth. The scent of the cooking meat in the cool, clean air was strong enough to activate the juices in White Wolf's mouth and belly. The smell of the white man was even stronger.

He had eaten little in the five days since the disastrous battle with the pony soldiers. A few early-winter rose berries. Some edible root vegetables, wild turnips he had dug up with a stick. A mouse's small cache of dried beans buried at an old campsite. Some acorns.

He was a renowned hunter, and he was not unarmed. He still had his knife, and on the second day after leaving the eagle's perch he had begun to fashion a tomahawk, which he now carried under his belt. It was a wedge-shaped stone secured to a sturdy length of branch by strips of leather he had cut from his shirt. But as winter had closed in, game was suddenly scarce. White Wolf had seen buffalo in the distance, and elk and deer, but he was wounded and on foot. He could not hope to approach them. For this he would have to make a bow. The rabbit outran him easily. Even the mouse laughed at his weakness, skittering out of reach and pausing to look back at him.

The poultice he had made of wild herbs for the great wound in his back had eased the pain, and the wound had long since ceased to bleed profusely. But it had festered now, and it was this poison that frightened the warrior far more than the wound itself, for it said that he had been contaminated with the spirit of evil that was always at war with good in every man.

White Wolf had begun to think of death.

Death was a close familiar to the warriors of the plains, especially one who had ridden into as many battles and passed through the cycle of as many changing seasons as White Wolf. And there were times now when he knew that he was not afraid to walk the Trail of the Spirits.

He had seen many of his friends die in battle. In the Land of Many Lodges a host of his ancestors waited for him, gathered around the main circle of the camp. White Wolf knew that this place was a good land where there was always plentiful game to hunt. An old one like himself, a Big

Belly who had known much honor and glory, did not fear death so much as the manner of dying.

It would have been good if he had been slain in the hot fury of his charge into the ranks of the pony soldiers, even if his body had not been recovered. Some of the wise men argued that it was indeed good to fall and to remain unburied in the territory of the enemy. White Wolf was not sure of this, for the white man could not be trusted not to mutilate the body of the fallen warrior, even a very brave one.

It was better to die in battle than to live to walk with a cane, an old one who could no longer fight, a toothless wolf who boasted only of the past.

But all of this was idle, for he had lived through his last battle with the soldiers. He had escaped when he could no longer fight, when he had neither bow nor rifle and he had been wounded. And in escaping he had counted coup on the white chief. That memory had succored him while he lay hidden on the eagle's ledge until the searchers went away without finding him.

He had survived. But now the evil was inside him, entering through his wound, and it was an enemy more mysterious and more terrifying than any white soldier.

White Wolf crept closer to the campfire, silent as the snow that fell over his shoulders and upon his head, the snow that lay on the ground and across the branches of the trees and over the bushes, muffling all sound as it stifled the smells of the earth.

The *wasicu* sensed no danger. He sat motionless, hunched close to his fire, smoking the white man's pipe. The smell of the burning tobacco was good to White Wolf, almost as tempting as the smell of the burning meat the enemy had eaten while White Wolf watched in hunger.

He was a tall man, taller even than White Wolf himself. A thick, close stubble of beard blackened his lean, angular face. Sometimes, when moving about his camp, he seemed to hold himself stiffly and awkwardly, as if he were in pain. But there was no sign of any wound. After watching him for more than an hour, White Wolf felt that he knew many things about this enemy. He was a patient, self-contained man. He was a hunter, as familiar with the earth and the sky as an Indian. There was anger in him, revealed in his brooding stare into his fire, but it was not the sour, pervasive anger White Wolf had seen so often in the faces of white men. He was armed with rifle, six-gun, and a broad-bladed knife— weapons White Wolf coveted. More important than any of these factors, he was a formidable man. And it was this that caused White Wolf to ponder his move carefully.

Under other circumstances he would not have hesitated. He would have waited only for the right moment before he attacked. But the sickness that had entered into his wound was a terrible burden to carry into any battle. He must acknowledge his weakness. The *wasicu*'s weapons were to be desired, but there was something far more important, upon which White Wolf's very life now depended.

The white man's horses.

There were two: a sorrel, which had been hobbled and left free to graze, and a deep-chested mare the color of a muddy river bottom. This horse, clearly larger and stronger, must be the white man's favorite. He had not only hobbled her but also secured her to a picket line, as if to make certain that she would not be stolen.

This was the horse White Wolf had now determined to steal.

He waited just beyond the feeble ring of light cast out by the enemy's fire, as still as a tree stump upon which the powdery snow fell unnoticed. He would wait until the white man slept.

Such a horse would carry him far and fast, he thought, swift as the wind. It would bring him new honor to ride such a horse into his village, a horse taken from the enemy. He had won many honors in his long life, but this would please him as much as any in the past.

At last the white man rolled himself into his blanket and lay close to the fire's warmth. He had his revolver out of its holster, White Wolf saw, lying close to his hand under the edge of the blanket. The knowledge banished any lingering question in the Indian warrior's mind over attacking the enemy while he slept.

This one would sleep lightly.

White Wolf's stomach growled noisily, hungry as a dog. It seemed as if he could still smell the meat cooking over the fire, its odor mingling with the wood smoke that still drifted to him in the cold stillness of the night. This was the Moon of the Hairless Calves, which was also called the Frost Moon. Two of the buffalo cows his hunting party had butchered had carried the hairless fetuses. Suddenly he wondered if he would live to see again the time when the calves were born and the croaking of the frog was heard once more in the streams and valleys. That was the best time for his people, the end of the long winter, the beginning of new life. Would it be so for him?

The thought was a strange one in the old warrior's mind. He examined it with wonder.

For another hour after the white man no longer stirred in his blankets White Wolf waited, indifferent to the stiffness of his bones. Unexpectedly, he slept.

He dreamed of a great herd of buffalo, stretching across the plain as numerous as the grasses. The sun was warm and the wind was soft, whispering in the long grass its ancient songs. Many of the shaggy beasts were rolling in a broad pit they had made with their bodies, their coats thick with mud. The great bulk of the herd moved slowly, grazing. As far as the eye could see across that rolling prairie there was nothing to frighten the buffalo. Where were the hunters? What had become of them?

There was no one to hear the wind's song in the grass. Though the prairie teemed with life, there was a terrible sense of emptiness, of loss, as if the hunters had forever been banished. Against the molten sky a lone eagle soared high, but as far as the eagle could see there was not a single hunter.

White Wolf jerked awake, shivering. He had lost his dew clothes when he had had to abandon his horse. His deerskin shirt was thin protection against the deepening cold. But it was not this that caused him to shiver. It was . . .

He shook his head. The dream fled from him.

The white man lay as before in his blankets. The fire had dimmed to a small pocket of glowing ashes. Sometimes White Wolf could hear the faint hissing of snowflakes landing on the embers.

Cautiously he slipped through the brush toward the two horses. The smaller one had moved away, though not far enough to be out of sight. The big mud-colored mare remained picketed at the edge of the clearing. White Wolf made no sound—less than the trickling of the nearby creek. He did not hesitate now. He did not search for the picket, but sliced through the line quickly with his knife.

The mare shied nervously away from him, disturbed by his unfamiliar smell. Moving close, White Wolf patted her gently. He ran his hands along her flanks and up and down her legs, across her back and neck, soothing her, making the animal aware that she was his to touch and command. His groping hands found a loose halter. He tested and tightened it to his liking. When the mare seemed to have quieted down he carefully released her hobbled front legs. Her nostrils flared, her breath steaming in the cold air.

White Wolf peered toward the sleeping enemy. He had not moved.

There was a faint reluctance over leaving the man's sleep undisturbed, his weapons unclaimed, but White Wolf shrugged it off. The path of wisdom recognized realities, not the dreams of youth.

Gathering his strength, he vaulted onto the big horse's back.

For a moment the mare fought the pull of the rope with her jaws and neck. Her ears folded against her head. Flattened low over the horse's neck with one hand digging into her mane and his knees tight against her flanks, White Wolf felt a tug of surprise over the unexpectedly stubborn resistance.

79

Then the hard-packed mass of bone and muscle beneath him exploded like a thunderclap.

For a brief moment, astonished, pain erupting in his body as the big horse bucked and jumped through tangled brush, White Wolf hung on with instinctive skill.

The mare leaped into the open of the clearing. Sprays of snow flew from her hoofs like dust. With a twisting jump she jarred him loose, and threw him.

White Wolf tumbled across the open, leaving a white wake behind. Buckled with pain, he tried to straighten and rise, but his body would not obey him. His wild, stunned eyes searched for and found the place where the enemy had slept just as the white man's gun crashed and a stream of flame stabbed through the darkness toward him.

12

The sudden crashing of a big animal through the underbrush jolted Lee Crosswhite awake, his hand grabbing for the butt of his revolver. A bear, he thought with alarm, and it was a moment before his sleep-dulled mind told him that it was late in the season for a bear to be hunting.

Then the big claybank mare burst into the clearing. Amazement shocked him awake like a cold water plunge. The apparition on the mare's back was hardly real, but a part of his mind told him it was. The claybank bucked, jumping halfway across the clearing. The Indian flew over her head.

By then Crosswhite was fully alert, registering the danger, understanding in a flash what had happened: the attempt to steal a horse, the natural assumption that the big mare was broken to a rider, the thief's consternation when the horse bucked. He snapped a shot at the boiling little cloud of leather and color and snow.

The Indian came to rest at the far edge of the clearing. Crosswhite thumbed back the hammer of his gun, aiming more carefully.

At the last instant he hesitated.

The Indian stirred feebly on his back but did not rise. Surprise nudged Crosswhite a step closer.

He had been sure his first hasty shot had missed. Then the Indian moved, and he saw a streak of red defiling the snow.

He had been hit in the back. He was bleeding.

Relaxing slightly, Crosswhite approached the fallen man warily. His gaze confirmed the telltale darkness on the snow. He eased the hammer of his gun down. His first surprise was now returning. Where had this redskin come from? Was he alone? Was he only after a horse? Why hadn't he tried to slit Crosswhite's throat while he slept?

"Looks like you latched onto more hell than you could handle," he muttered aloud.

The Indian's dark eyes were open, staring at him. Crosswhite thought he could read pain in them, though he could not be sure. The blocky, bold-featured, impassive face told him nothing. Looking for a gun, Crosswhite saw none. That explained why the devil hadn't *shot* him while he slept. But it still didn't explain . . .

He had lowered his gun, but he stepped too close. A hand shot out to seize his ankle. Before he could react, Crosswhite felt himself skidding off his feet. He slammed onto his back. Somehow his thumb had found the hammer once more as he fell, and his finger tightened on the trigger automatically. The six-shooter kicked in his hand, and a wild shot plowed a furrow through the snow.

A writhing weight fell across him—leather and

sweat and something foul, sick. He grappled with the Indian. A tomahawk flashed above his head. Stone thudded into the frozen ground inches from his ear. Crosswhite clubbed frantically with the barrel of his gun. It struck bone.

Fingers were at his throat, digging like claws, trying to cut through his flesh, choking him.

Suddenly the grip eased. The Indian sagged. Crosswhite gave a violent, twisting shove and the other man toppled off him with surprising ease. He struggled clear, whipping up his gun.

For the second time something stopped his trigger finger before it squeezed.

This time the Indian did not move at all.

He was wounded, sure enough, but Crosswhite did not need to inspect the wound closely or in good light to realize that it was at least a few days old. His own shot, as he had guessed, had missed the mark.

That explained the Indian's weakness, the feeble effort at a fight—although that single blow with the tomahawk had come close to splitting Crosswhite's skull.

Wounded, he thought. And armed only with that crude club and a knife.

If he'd tried to steal the sorrel he would have escaped clean. Not that it would have mattered in the long run. Not with that festering wound. He would not have ridden far.

Although the warrior was apparently no longer any threat to him, Crosswhite took the precaution of binding his wrists and ankles with rope, running a length of the line between the knots at wrists and ankles. Then he waited for daylight.

By dawn the Indian was in delirium, occasionally thrashing around so violently that Crosswhite wondered about the need or wisdom of keeping him tied up. He cut the line joining hands and feet but left the other bonds in place. Out of compassion he had thrown a blanket over the unconscious man, who kept getting tangled in it. Crosswhite straightened it out once more. For a spell the Indian talked wildly, words that Crosswhite could not follow with his meager knowledge of the Sioux tongue. Then he relapsed into silence.

Crosswhite built up his fire and heated coffee. He chewed some of the dried meat and hard biscuits—they were going stale now—that Wishbone Hines' widow woman had pressed upon him, perhaps out of belated qualms over denying him welcome under his old friend's roof. Sipping the hot brew, from which clouds of steam rose into the crisp, clear morning that had followed the snowfall, he studied his prisoner.

He was an old-timer, Crosswhite judged, though it was generally hard to tell the age of an Indian precisely. The hair, on close inspection, was more iron-gray than black. It was gathered into two long braids, both of which bore fur-trimmed braid wraps. The strong face was typically Sioux—eyes set wide apart over high, broad cheekbones, nose long and wide and heavily bridged, chin like a vise. The whole seamed and stitched like old leather. The old man's body, tall and big-framed, was still sinewy with muscle, but the skin gathered in places that betrayed his age, and he was thick around the middle.

One of the Big Bellies. A warleader, a chief.

What little the Indian wore seemed to confirm this judgment. His feet were clad in high-ankled moccasins. His leggings were richly ornamented with quills, and each bore distinctive black crosses, the mark earned only by saving a fellow warrior's hide in battle. His deerskin shirt bore two bands of quillwork across the shoulders and bands on each arm. And along both arms was the hair fringe worn only by important chiefs.

Crosswhite speculated over his identity. He had thought that most of the leaders of the great plains tribes had gone into the reservations, although Sitting Bull was supposed to be sitting safely up in Canada, where the U. S. Army couldn't get at him.

And how had this one been shot in the back? In a fight with his own kind? Or in a clash with his white enemies, cattleman or soldier?

For a while the Indian moved restlessly, muttering an occasional unintelligible word or phrase. Sweat beaded his forehead in spite of the cold. Then he slept again.

When he woke his dark eyes were clear, alert with intelligence. They discovered Crosswhite almost instantly. "*Wasicu*," he said. The enemy.

"And you're a horse thief," Crosswhite said.

The Indian tested the rope around his wrists and ankles. Even that small effort cost him, and he fell back, spent.

"Who are you?" Crosswhite asked. There was no answer. "You understand any white man talk?"

The old warrior merely stared at him, his face without expression, his eyes stony. That ugly wound in his back was eating him alive, Crosswhite thought, but he would never let it show.

"Might as well talk," Crosswhite said mildly. "I'm not the enemy."

"*Wasicu*," the chief repeated. "You are the enemy."

"Now we're back where we started. You got a name?"

He thought the warrior was going to ignore the question again, but at length he spoke. "I am of the Lakotas," he said.

The Lakotas. The Men. Well, they could call themselves that with some justification, Crosswhite thought. He was not an Indian-hater, though he had fought them more than once. In

86

battle they had earned his respect, and it seemed like they were no more guilty of atrocities than the white soldiers they fought.

He could get no more out of the wounded man, and soon gave up trying.

In the early afternoon the sky turned leaden with the threat of a renewed storm. He ought to be moving, Crosswhite thought, hunched over the fire he had built up. What the hell did he think he was doing, nursing a dying Indian? Likely if he waited too long he would have to dig his way through to Cheyenne City.

But something a lot stronger than concern over the weather held him there. Maybe it was the stoic dignity of the old chief. He was an arrogant old son-of-a-bitch, but he had courage and dignity. He wouldn't let pain show, and he wouldn't complain. He wouldn't shake his fist at the sky and holler about his luck.

Lakota. He was a Man, right enough. You had to give him that. And somehow it didn't seem right to ride off and leave him there for the wolves, even if you knew that was exactly what he would have done if their roles had been reversed.

Crosswhite boiled some water with roots and pieces of dried meat in it to make a broth. The Indian seemed to take a little of it, but he was weaker. There was an odd brightness in his dark eyes, the shine of fever. When he was conscious he alternated between lucid periods when he looked at Crosswhite with recognition and understanding, and other moments when he muttered wildly or even tried to struggle.

Late in the day Crosswhite cut the ropes that secured the Indian's wrists and feet. Such precautions had become pointless.

It was during one of his intervals of delirium that the old warrior spoke a name clearly in English: White Wolf. Crosswhite moved quickly to his side, bending close, feeling both surprise and a touch of awe. "Are you White Wolf?" he asked. "Is that what you're saying?"

The Indian mumbled in his own language, and Crosswhite swore over his own feeble knowledge of that tongue. The dying man might simply have uttered the name of his chief, or his more famous brother or cousin who would come to avenge him. But if the name was his own . . .

Crosswhite remembered now that White Wolf was one of the renegades. Feeling betrayed over an earlier peace treaty he had signed with the white chiefs, he had refused to have any more parlaying with them. Crosswhite had supposed him caught long before this, like most of the others. Apparently that assumption was wrong— if this was indeed White Wolf.

The supposition gave more weight to the possibility that he had been wounded in a skirmish with the U. S. Cavalry, although the Indian seemed to have wandered far afield. For some time now the Indians had steered clear of the cattle country.

Maybe because he was wounded. Maybe they were hunting him down.

The Indian warrior had one more period of intelligence before nightfall. His eyes seemed less hostile, but Crosswhite guessed that what he read in them was puzzlement rather than gratitude. The Sioux warrior expected no quarter from his enemies, and gave none. A stubborn maverick like White Wolf wouldn't know what to make of a lone cowhand feeding him broth after he had tried to steal a horse and kill its owner. There were times when Crosswhite questioned the sense of it himself.

Later the old man talked, but he was no longer aware of the presence of his enemy. The words were of his mind and heart, and Crosswhite wished he knew more of them. Some he recognized. The elk and the buffalo. The circle of tipis. The coming of spring. And—with feverish excitement—words of battle. Pony soldiers. Guns. A surprise attack in the first light of dawn.

Crosswhite wondered if he was dreaming of his last battle, or of glories still to come.

During the night the Lakota warrior died. Crosswhite had no certain knowledge of his identity, and he could hardly claim to have been the old man's brother. Yet he felt saddened. The death of any brave man was something to notice.

He remembered that many of White Wolf's people believed in burial above ground, leaving them free to move about along the spirit trail after death, searching for the camp of their ancestors. With the ground as hard as it was, Crosswhite couldn't have dug much of a grave, anyway. The frozen ground also made him dubious about erecting a burial scaffold such as he had seen at the site of abandoned Sioux villages, and occasionally in the middle of the prairie in lonely isolation. How would he make the supporting stakes secure if he couldn't drive them into the ground?

He searched for an alternative. Prowling west of the creek where he had camped, he came to the mouth of a canyon. Within its high protecting walls grew a tall pine whose large bottom branches were more than six feet above the canyon floor. In these branches, which formed a natural scaffold of sorts, Crosswhite cradled the Indian's body. Then he spent an hour hunting for rocks, thorny bushes, and brambles to pile around the base of the tree, creating a thick and painful barrier to discourage animals from trying to climb the tree or reach the body by jumping. More than once, as a thorn or sharp branch pierced his gloves and raked his arms, he swore at himself for a fool. But he persisted until he was satisfied.

He left the dead chief's tomahawk and knife

with him, along with the small pouch of "medicine" attached to his belt. That was all there was. Not much to take with him to that other hunting ground, Crosswhite thought.

He shook himself, angry without knowing exactly why.

As he rode away, stubbornly resisting looking back, he was aware for the first time that the sky had darkened, and it began to snow.

13

The snow, the first severe storm of that winter, followed Lee Crosswhite all the way into Cheyenne City. By the time he caught his first glimpse of the clustered buildings of the town, their thick new white roofs seen through a curtain of whirling flakes, the blowing drifts were piling as high as a horse's shoulder points. The cold had turned bitter, made more fierce by howling winds.

That cold wind was a searching wind. It was the kind that blew through every crack in the tightest shelter. It found every opening in a man's clothes. It touched his fingers and his toes with the black dread of frostbite. Just as it discovered every torn place or crack in his coat and gloves and boots, it searched out any weakness in the man himself and cut right through to his bones.

Hunched over as he bore into that wind, Crosswhite felt the accumulation of this winter's blows piling up on him like snow on a weakened roof. It had started with a piece of foolishness, as such cycles often did—the fool prank of Oakes and Spud that resulted in cracked bones for Crosswhite and the loss of a winter job. His own recklessness compounded the situation, letting him gamble away his wages. Picking a fight with Sut Rossiter at that time hadn't exactly been the pinnacle of wisdom either. Then, depriving him of at least temporary welcome, there was the unexpected marriage of Wishbone Hines to a woman with a nearly grown daughter she wasn't going to leave alone with any penniless drifter. Once a string of bad luck like that got started, it seemed like there was no stopping it. You could rail against it, but that had about as much effect as hollering at the wind, which simply grabbed your words and scattered them before they could be heard.

He wasn't much better off than that dead Indian, Crosswhite brooded as he rode. It looked like this was a battle he wasn't supposed to win. Even when that sick old man found a horse he thought would carry him off safe to his people, it turned out to be the one horse in a thousand he could have picked on any white man's string that wouldn't tolerate a rider of any kind. Why, as long as such a run of luck was playing out, Crosswhite would be crazy to call down on a gunslick like Sut Rossiter.

The thought would not make him flinch from that confrontation, but it did produce a certain gloom over the probable outcome.

Seeing Cheyenne City brought relief and an immediate lifting of Crosswhite's spirits. He wasn't going to be buried under a snowdrift after all, and Rossiter's bullet wouldn't put him under either.

And the loneliness that had been pressing in on him would soon be over. Crosswhite grinned, tasting light flakes of snow against his teeth and tongue. Good old Annie, he thought. There were more ways than one for a man to keep warm when the cold wind howled.

Annie Macauley had known Lee Crosswhite for more years than she was willing to count. But "known" did not exactly say it. During all those years he was not the only man she had known. He *was* the only man she had loved.

She wasn't about to tell him that, certainly not in so many words. When he appeared suddenly at her door, coming out of the dusk of that snowy winter evening like an apparition, she didn't try to hide her delight, but she knew better than to let him see the pain that accompanied her sudden joy, the pain that was part of having a man and not having him, of loving a man you knew could give as much love in return if he ever stopped looking over the next horizon.

In her heart Annie did not believe that Lee Crosswhite would ever stop looking. That made her a silly woman for loving him the way she did, and for dreaming, but she would never let him see that.

Instead, she threw herself into his big bear

hug—she did not see him wince—and pressed her warm cheek against the icy stubble of his beard. Those cold barbs were a week or more old, and his lips were cool and tasted of snow.

"Lee Crosswhite! I thought you'd hibernated for sure. Oh, golly, it's good to see you."

She could see how pleased he was by the warmth of her greeting. "You're a sight for winter-sore eyes yourself, girl. Get back in there out of the cold. You've let me get snow all over you."

"And you look like the original snowman. Are you certain some kids didn't roll you together out there, making a couple of big snowballs and putting that hat on 'em?"

"That's what I feel like." He stamped his boots on the porch, trying to shed some of the snow before he stepped into the warm brightness of the house. "Maybe I'll just melt here inside, just turn into a big puddle."

She laughed, elation swelling in her heart like a huge bubble. Dear God, she thought, how is it that he can make me feel like this after all these years, just walking in out of the snow after being away half the year, and never a word in between times?

"Well, if you're gonna melt," she said, "come into the kitchen where it's easier to mop up. Give me that coat. And you'd better take those wet boots off. For heaven's sake, where did you come from? How long have you been in town?"

"I just this minute rode in," Crosswhite said, grinning at her with the easy pleasure shared by two old friends. "Took time to stable my horses, that's all, and come right over to see you."

"Now you're trying to flatter me 'cause you didn't even stop at the saloon."

"Well, if that don't flatter you, girl, then I guess nothin' will. I tell you it's *cold* out there."

She didn't have to fetch up a smile at his broad hint. There was a kind of permanent smile plastered all over her face. Stop grinning at him, she admonished herself. He isn't Tristan or Lancelot or any of those gallants, he's only a rolling cowhand the wind blew in, and he'll blow out again just as suddenly.

But the smile stayed. After all, he *had* come straight to her from the stables. If he'd stopped at the Red Garter or the Wagon Wheel or Pike's Hotel Saloon she would have smelled the whisky on his breath when she kissed him.

That counted for something, didn't it?

He stood in front of the wood stove in the kitchen to warm himself, rubbing his hands over the fire at first, then turning his back to it, facing her. He moved stiffly, she thought, as if he were getting older and felt the cold in his bones. Well, they were neither of them getting any younger. But as recently as last spring she had known that the fire that was in Crosswhite still burned high, the need to test himself, the eagerness to search for whatever it was that called to him (not that he really knew himself what it was), the necessity to be in the open and heading somewhere, as free as a deer in the forest or a bird in the sky, chattel to no man—or woman.

"Here," she said, handing him a tumbler generously filled with the good whisky she kept for these infrequent times. "This'll warm you."

"Just seein' you again warms me, girl. Besides, you got a good fire goin' in this here stove."

"You couldn't just let it be me, could you?"

Crosswhite laughed. "You're drinkin' with me, ain't you, Annie? After all, this is some sort of a celebration."

"Is that what it is?"

"That's what it is, girl," he declared, his eyes becoming suddenly serious. "You know that. Hell's fire, I don't have to tell you that, not after all the years we been celebratin' together."

She did not remind him how little they were together. Instead, she poured whisky into a glass for herself. "You don't think I'd slight myself, do you?"

He grinned again, clinked his glass against hers, and drank. His gaze held warm upon hers, and she thought, oh golly, I'm the one who's gonna melt when he looks at me like that, not him. His presence filled the room for her. She peered intently at his face, trying to search behind the beard for any sign of hurt that hadn't been there before, for any change at all. And something *was* there. Was it only the darkness of fatigue under his eyes?

"What's wrong?" he asked gently. "Ain't you glad to see me?"

"You know I am."

She moved to him once more, impulsively hugging him. This time she saw the pain that tugged at his eyes. "Lee! What's wrong? You're hurting!"

"Not so much if you'll stop squeezin' so hard."

"What's happened to you? Tell me!"

He shrugged it off. "Got throwed by a mean old claybank, that's all. Maybe put a wrinkle or two in this here shoulder and bumped some ribs. Nothin' that won't heal. I'm comin' along fine, girl. I take back what I said about you squeezin'. You go right ahead."

"I'd like to shoot that horse."

"She's right over in that stable waitin', but I'd appreciate it if you didn't shoot her just yet. I got a score to settle with her. After all, she did me out of a whole winter's wages at the Rocking-S."

Annie Macauley felt the bubble burst. The light in her eyes went dim, but Crosswhite failed to notice. "How . . . how did she do that? Oh. You mean . . . throwing you."

"Sure enough. But hell's fire, I reckon I'm just

as glad it happened now. Give me a chance to find you again, girl."

Annie smiled back, hiding the hurt once more because there was nothing else she could do. He didn't even realize how he had made her sound like an afterthought.

"I got to tell you, though, I coulda used those wages. My pockets is thin, girl. I ain't carryin' any extra weight at all."

She seized on that, not questioning what had happened to his summer's wages, telling herself that she was being selfish asking him to do without work he needed. With an effort she turned up the light once more in her eyes, making sure that he saw it.

Crosswhite cleared his throat. "Been a long time, Annie," he said. His voice was husky.

"Yes. A long time, Lee."

"My feet'll be cold."

"Won't be the first time. And they'll warm up soon enough."

"You'll see to that."

"Yes, I'll see to that, Mr. Snowman. Maybe I'll even give you a hot water bottle."

"That ain't what I had in mind."

"You snowmen are all the same."

"You're not," he said with that seriousness he could sometimes show without warning. "No one like you, Annie-girl. No one like you anywheres, and I been lookin'."

"I'll bet you have." But he had said the right thing, the only right thing. She opened the gates and let all the pleasure of having him back wash through her, the joy of wanting and needing and, if only for a short time, having.

14

Annie Macauley had met Lee Crosswhite in Denver City nearly six years before. She had been a singer and dancer with a troupe visiting that territorial capital, and Crosswhite had been in the audience one night at the opera house. She was then twenty-two years old, a small, pretty young woman with chestnut hair and unusually direct brown eyes.

The night Crosswhite saw her onstage was the last time she danced. A short flight of stairs and a small platform backstage collapsed while Annie was midway on the steps. Her leg was caught in the splintering shafts of wood. The large tendon behind her left ankle was severed.

That night two tall hats were passed around the local saloons. One of those hats was Crosswhite's, and he was one of the men who brought the collection of gold and silver to Annie's bedside the next day. "I only did it so's I could be sure you noticed me," he had often told her. To which she always answered, "You surely do know the way to a woman's heart."

If she was bitter over the abrupt end to her days as a dancer, she had never voiced that bitterness where Crosswhite could hear her. One of the things he liked in her, that always brought him back to her, was the toughness she had shown then and later, the uncomplaining acceptance of what had happened and the forthright decision to make her own way in the rough western territory.

The money from those two hats had brought her to Cheyenne City, a fledgling town that boomed after the Black Hills gold discoveries, and was now enjoying a second strike from the burgeoning business of cattle ranching. Annie had set up a small millinery and yardage goods store, selling ladies' hats and dresses, ribbons and lace and fabrics. If some men in the beginning had nudged each other with their elbows and grinned over her enterprise, now, in this winter of 1878, no one was laughing at her any more.

Lee Crosswhite walked her to her store through the piled-up snow on the morning after his return. The storm had passed and the town had an unreal brilliance, caught between the white glitter of the snow and the blue brightness of the sky. The clear, cold air made her nose and lungs sting when she breathed. It was like a Christmas picture, she thought, everything with a fresh shine to it, nothing dirty or hard or mean.

On the way Crosswhite questioned her about activities in and about Cheyenne City that winter, showing particular interest in the names of strangers who had come and gone. Annie would have found nothing strange in this interest if she wasn't remembering the way he strapped on his six-shooter before they set out, and the stubborn set of his jaw. Men generally wore guns, but there had been something purposeful in Crosswhite's actions and manner. He had said nothing in explanation, and she knew that it would do no good to pry into whatever was bothering him. He would tell her when he was ready, if at all.

At the entrance to her shop he left her with a brief smile and a few words, his thoughts elsewhere. She could not be sure if he was scowling against the morning glare or from those thoughts. She watched him kick his way through the boardwalk drifts with an apprehension that was perhaps out of keeping with any evidence.

Joy and fear, she thought. He brings you both. The fear was something she lived with every spring or summer when he rode off—the fear that she would never see him again, that he would go so far beyond the next mountain that it would be too far to come back, or that something would happen to him and she would never learn of it, never even hear what his fate was.

But that day he returned, in good humor, saying nothing important about what he had done, nothing to explain the hard scowl or the purposeful way he had checked the hang and fit of his gunbelt that morning.

On the third day after his return Crosswhite had to ask her for money. Immediately she realized that it had taken him that long to bring himself to the point of asking. Contrite, she tried to press more than the dollar he had asked into his hand. "No," he said. "It ain't right. You work hard for it."

They settled for the dollar, and her insistence on stopping by Ed Walsh's Livery Stables to pay something against the feed bill for Crosswhite's two horses. This would be a loan.

"I been thinkin' of selling the saddle," Crosswhite mused. "And maybe that sorrel, too, if I can find a buyer will pay the right price."

"Why not the dun?"

Crosswhite grinned. "Not yet."

"You *are* stubborn, Lee Crosswhite. Anyway, I won't hear of you selling your saddle and the only horse you have to ride. You know you don't have to do that, honey."

"Well, now, I can't rightly let you support me," he said gently. "This time of year there ain't nothin' around here to herd except the snow, and it won't last long if the sun keeps shining."

"That doesn't matter," she said.

But it did matter to him. The restlessness she could see in him made her uneasy. She was already looking forward with pleasure to having him with her at Christmas. She didn't want him to get a sudden urge to head south somewhere on the hope of finding winter work.

But he had no intention of leaving. That determination had little to do with her, as she was to learn at the end of that first week Crosswhite stayed with her. There wasn't much that pushed a man harder than his pride, and Crosswhite's pride had been more badly battered than his ribs.

It was Saturday night. He had been gone most of the afternoon and evening, prowling the town. He wasn't at the house on time for the supper she had prepared, and he made no apology when he made his belated appearance at her door. There was whisky on his breath and anger in his mood. "Looks like he ain't comin' after all," he muttered.

"Who?"

Crosswhite shrugged. He had laced the black coffee she poured for him with whisky. She hated these black moods in him, although in her experience they were rarer than in most men. It seemed to her that men were most often angry at something in themselves, some lack that moved them to self-contempt and an anger that covered it. Crosswhite had mostly been a stranger to such emotions.

Maybe it had something to do with what had been prodding him since his return.

"I hear there's a mighty important man came in on the afternoon train," Annie said. "Man named Hubbard."

"That so?" Crosswhite grunted without interest.

"Came all the way from Washington, they say. It's in the paper, all about how he's organizing an expedition to find some Indian chief." Crosswhite read laboriously, and she knew he would not have struggled through the paper. When he was in a better mood he liked to have her read to him or tell him the news, but now he was not really listening.

"Probably want to sign another treaty so they can break it," Crosswhite said, his scorn surprising her.

"No, that isn't—"

"He ain't comin'!" Crosswhite exploded abruptly. "That don't figger, but it must be so."

"Lee Crosswhite, if you don't tell me what you're talking about, and what's making you so techy—"

The sharpness of her tone caused him to look at her. "Rossiter," he said. "That man I asked you about. He's the one I am lookin' for."

"Why? What's so important about him?" Then, unkindly, stung by his attitude, "Does he owe you money?"

Crosswhite blinked slowly. She wasn't sure if her taunt had angered him, and her lips tightened in self-disgust. She wasn't going to keep him around long if she nattered at him.

Then he told her about Sut Rossiter, the lost wages, and the crooked deck. When he recounted details of the fight laconically, she felt herself flinching over each kick or blow, and the heat of sympathetic rage rose into her cheeks. "He should he whipped!" she cried without thinking.

Crosswhite smiled thinly. "I had somethin' like that in mind."

The very real danger struck her belatedly. "But . . . oh, golly, Lee, you said he was a gunman."

"Some say that."

"You can't . . . he'll kill you!"

"Maybe. But he won't kick me around this time. Not unless he kills me first."

Her fear came back in a rush, the constant fear of losing him, losing even the little she had of him. "Don't do it, honey. Let it go. It's not something to get yourself shot over."

"You know I can't do that," he said quietly.

15

That night they made love as if it were the last time. When it was over Crosswhite studied her with something like wonder in his eyes. After a while he said, "We been good together, girl."

"Yes."

"Long time."

"Yes."

She knew when not to say too much, he thought. That was a rare quality in a woman.

He thought about the hard loneliness of this winter, a loneliness unrelieved until now. A man like him didn't ask for much, but it seemed like he'd been facing a cold deck all along until Annie Macauley took a hand in the game. Maybe a man had to endure a bad winter before he would take a look at himself and where he was heading.

It wasn't gold Crosswhite had dreamed of so much, nor owning things, nor bossing a crew to make himself feel big and important, nor lifting the skirts of every Lilly Langtry who stepped out on the stage and showed him an ankle. What in hell was it, then? A man would have to be crazy to say that he yearned to feed on all the dust a cowhand had to breathe and swallow. He'd have to be a fool not to know there was better whisky somewhere to drink than the rotgut served over the bar in any cowtown saloon. He would have had to be kicked in the head somewhere along the line to believe that rope-burned hands and saddle-sore loins and empty pockets added up to cowboy heaven.

He had wanted space around him. Freedom to stretch himself and yell as loud as he wanted sometimes without anyone to tell him no. The knowledge that he could saddle up and ride away any time he chose, along any trail that beckoned to him. Friends. A full belly most of the time.

Hell, it wasn't much, but it seemed like all the promises had withered. Everything you wanted to see or touch or try turned out to be less than you'd been told. A horse dumped you into a rail and you were finished. Like some Indians leaving their old ones out to die when they were too slow to follow, too weak to contribute. Was that what it all came down to?

He thought suddenly of the old warrior he had buried in the arms of the tree at the mouth of the canyon. His hopes had withered, too, long before he took a bullet in the back. He hadn't wanted much either, just the chance to hunt his buffalo and smoke his pipe and acquit himself well in battle with the old enemies of his people, the Shoshones maybe or some Crows. He'd seen it all go, and at the end all he'd had beside him was some white man as solitary as himself to preside over his death and to wish him well wherever he was going.

You couldn't even count on old friends staying the same. "You remember Wishbone Hines?" he asked suddenly.

"Wishbone? Little sawed-off gent with legs that wouldn't come together?"

"That's him."

"Sure, I remember him. You used to ride together."

"Used to." Yes, that said it plain. "He got himself married."

"He did?" Annie showed her amazement. "I can hardly believe it." She rolled her head away from Crosswhite on the feather pillow. I don't want to hear about it, she thought. Not right now.

"It's true enough. To a widow woman. I stopped by there, at this little spread he's got, that he was always bragging about, but I didn't stay."

"Why not? I'm sure his . . . wife would have made you welcome."

"Well . . ." He decided it might be best not to make too much of that nubile young daughter. "She made all the right sounds, but I reckon she was scared I might talk old Wishbone into chasin' the buffalo."

"Oh, Lee, that's not likely."

"Didn't want any no-account saddlebum hangin' around."

"You're not no-account. Don't let me hear you talk that way." Her eyes were oddly moist, he thought, puzzled. She turned her head again, and in the darkness he was not sure if he had imagined tears. "A saddlebum, maybe, but not no-account."

Crosswhite grinned. The smile faded before a rush of sentiment. Damned if Annie wasn't the only one who really cared about him. "Maybe we oughta get hitched," he blurted. The words were out before he really knew what he was going to say.

He felt her body stiffen. "Don't talk foolish," she said, the words muffled against her pillow.

"What's so foolish about it?" He felt a need to defend his unpremeditated proposal. "We get along, don't we?"

"That . . ."

"What did you say?"

She only shook her head, still not turning to face him.

"I ain't sayin' it's only getting along. I know it's more than that, for me the same as for you," he argued. "Hey, didn't you hear what I asked you, girl? I'm askin' you to marry me!"

She rolled onto her back and faced him then, the movement almost violent. Her eyes seemed huge and wet, and he realized that she was indeed crying. "Damn you, Lee Crosswhite! It's not me you want, it's a nice, warm, cozy place to sleep and a stove to warm your behind as long as there's nothing but snow outside and no place for you to ride."

"I thought you wanted—"

"You don't think at all! If you did you'd know I've wanted to hear those words every single day for the past five years or more, but I want you to mean them. You've always been honest with me, and I've accepted that. You never made me any promises. I knew how it was with you. Now you're not being honest any more, and I hate you for that, do you hear?"

"You're not makin' any sense."

"I'm making all the sense that's being spoke in this room. First time the sun stayed out for a week and your cards started to turn up you'd regret everything you said."

"You're tryin' to say I don't love you," he mumbled defensively. "You're wrong, Annie."

"Maybe you do care. God knows I've tried to tell myself you do. But not this way, Lee. Not when you'd wish you could take your words back in the morning, and I'd sit there watching you and knowing what you were wishing." For a moment she was silent. She seemed to be breathing hard, as if she had been running. He wanted to reach out and hold her, but something stopped him. She wasn't ready for that, not right now. "One minute you tell me you're going to go up against this Sut Rossiter, and the next minute you're asking me to marry you, just because Wishbone Hines has found himself a woman to keep the cold off and you didn't have one. Do you think I'll be better off being a widow?"

"Now look here, girl—"

"You tell me he's a gunfighter, and you're a long ways from being that. Still, you're going against him. Do you mean to give that up, now you want me for a wife?"

"No." He felt anger stirring at last in response to her anger.

"Then go to sleep!"

But he did not sleep for a long time. She lay rigid beside him, silent and remote, as if there were a wall between them. She did not move a muscle, but he was not sure at all if she was asleep or lying there in stiff rejection, her eyes big and dark and wet.

In the morning she seemed to act as if he had never spoken. He was not sure what he felt. There was a trace of anger, of lingering resentment over her reaction to his proposal, but there was also a guilty relief that he was reluctant to confess even to himself. She knew him better than he knew himself.

But when he had dressed and shuffled around the kitchen awkwardly after breakfast, fussing over her, at last she said, "I think you'd best find another place to stay, Lee. You'll be welcome at this table any time you're hungry, I want you to know that, but you can find another bed."

"Aw, now, Annie—"

"I mean it." There was a circle of high color in each of her cheeks. She was beautiful in her dignity and determination, he realized with a startled awe. "And if you think that means I don't love you, just come around in the spring and ask me that same question, Lee Crosswhite." It was a challenge, and they both knew it. "It doesn't even have to be the same question. All you have to do is ask me to wait. Just so's I know you mean it."

"Maybe I'll do that," he snapped back. "If I'm still alive. That seems to bother you."

"That's right." Her voice shook. "If you're still alive."

He wanted to take it all back, any words that could have hurt her so deeply, but it was too late for that. Hell's fire, he muttered savagely to himself. Who could ever learn to handle a woman? Then he stamped out into the cold gray of the morning.

16

Crosswhite's saddle was a big, heavy single rig, the kind that was called a three-quarter rig because the rings that caught the single cinch were set forward a little from center. In spite of the incident at the Rocking-S when his single cinch had been tampered with, Crosswhite still preferred this rig to the double-rig saddles that were being seen more and more on the northern ranges.

The saddle had a low cantle and a slick horn, which gave it its popular name: apple horn. It looked something like an apple cut in half, with the slender stem sticking up front. It had been made by a Texas saddlemaker, and Crosswhite had bought it from a down-and-out rider some two years before in Kansas. It was the most comfortable saddle Crosswhite had ever owned, and he would give it up reluctantly.

But he knew he had to. He was in about the same fix as that waddy he'd bought the saddle from. It was going to be a long, cold winter, and he was scraping bottom.

He couldn't go back to Annie's table with his hat in his hand, that was sure. Not after what had been said.

The hostler's name was Ed Walsh, although he

was always called—for some reason Crosswhite had never heard—Sweetwater. He'd been around these stables as long as Crosswhite could remember coming there.

Sweetwater greeted Crosswhite amiably, but he seemed to be surprisingly busy that morning, and it was several minutes before he took time out from brushing down a very handsome chestnut, a Sunday horse if Crosswhite had ever seen one. While waiting, Crosswhite took note of the unusual number of horses in the stalls or turned outside to paw around in the recent snow. He wondered at this sudden increase in population.

"They have got you jumpin'," he said when Sweetwater Walsh paused sociably.

"That's a fact." The hostler regarded him speculatively. His blue eyes had a loose lower lid, with a line of red showing the way it did on some hound dogs. He chewed tobacco, a wad of which he now shifted around in a leathery cheek. He had a drooping mustache, which evidently served as a strainer for his tobacco juice. "Nothin' I can't handle," he said.

It was his way of saying that there wasn't enough work for stray cowpunchers.

"You're better with a fork and brush than me," Crosswhite said. "I just come by to say that saddle of mine is available to the right buyer."

Two bristly gray eyebrows rose slightly. "It seems like a fine rig."

116

"Yeah."

"You sure you want to sell it?"

"I'm not celebrating over it," Crosswhite said. "But it's for sale, right enough."

Sweetwater Walsh considered this. At length he said, "You got two horses out there. Might be I could sell one of 'em."

Crosswhite slowly shook his head. He could ride the sorrel bareback if he had to, or with a piece of leather to sit on, like an Indian. He would have to be a lot hungrier before he would part with that horse, even though he had made the same suggestion himself to Annie Macauley.

The claybank was different. He wondered what it was that made him so stubborn about letting her go. She was of no use to him, unless you counted the way she had thrown that wounded Indian as a useful service. Saddle-broke or not, she would bring enough to keep him in grub for a spell.

He shook his head. Not yet, anyway. He wasn't up against that wall yet. "Just the saddle," he said. He added, "For now."

Sweetwater carefully aimed and spat a stream of juice that stained the dirty snow just beyond the stable doors with an orange streak. "Anythin' you say. Shouldn't be no trouble findin' a buyer, not when that Indian expedition is bein' organized."

"What expedition is that?"

"Some feller from back East. That's his horse

I been rubbin' down—a real fine horse. He is lookin' for riders to take on some kind of Injun hunt." Sweetwater paused briefly, as if weighing the wisdom of his next words. "Maybe you'd like to join up. Wouldn't have to sell your rig."

Crosswhite remembered Annie's comments about the story in the newspaper. A man from Washington, she had said, but he could remember little else. What was it the newspaper had called him? A famous entrepreneur. Crosswhite wasn't sure he could pronounce it right, much less say what it meant.

"I reckon I'd be better off sellin' my saddle than to go off huntin' Indians with some Easterner."

Sweetwater Walsh grinned. "Well, it ain't exactly any Injun he wants. He's after one Injun in particular, name of White Wolf."

The familiar name jarred Crosswhite. Instantly he thought of the old man he had buried in the tree, who had spoken that name aloud—and who was old enough to be the famous chief.

"Seems like the cavalry has been after that one for quite a spell," he said. "What makes this Easterner think he can find him?"

"Well, ain't you heard? They think maybe he's dead. Leastwise, that's what the story is. Seems the cavalry jumped White Wolf and some of his renegades 'bout a fortnight back, more or less. They're sure it was White Wolf hisself, and the claim is he got hisself shot."

"That should be easy enough to prove."

Sweetwater shook his head, enjoying the playing out of his story. "He got away. It seems like he rode right through them cavalry like the devil hisself, and then led 'em a chase before he disappeared. They're sure he was hurtin', though, and they got his horse to prove it. It's been quite a story hereabouts. I'm surprised you ain't heard of it."

"I been on the move. Out there." His nod took in the vast white emptiness to the west.

"Well, the word got all the way back to Washington, and stirred up all kinds of excitement. That's what brought this feller Hubbard on the run. There's some say White Wolf must be dead, that he was carryin' lead and on foot out there in the hills, and with all this snow and cold comin' on he wouldn't have much chance."

"Some Indians is stubborn about dyin'," Crosswhite said. His earlier speculation was beginning to turn into conviction. That old horse thief was not only the right age and stature of man. He had also been shot in the back. He could have ridden through cavalry lines and taken a bullet in the back while he made his escape.

And he had been on foot when he came to Crosswhite's camp.

White Wolf. One of the tough old renegades, as Sweetwater Walsh had called him. Wouldn't stick his head into the halter for anything.

Crosswhite felt a brief but strong satisfaction over what he had done for the dying Indian, even though he had had misgivings at the time. Hell, it was something, just having run into a scalphunter like that one. It made him feel like . . . he wasn't sure. Like the first time you ever had a bear in your sights maybe, that first time, and you were struck with a kind of awe for the huge animal, an admiration of its wild strength, a feeling so strong that it was a weight holding back the squeeze of your trigger finger. Dropping him brought a mixture of emotions, a surging pride diluted by sadness.

Crosswhite felt the inadequacy of his grasp of words, a feeling fresh from Annie Macauley's recounting of the newspaper story, which he had not wanted much to hear because of its reminder that most of the world of print was beyond him, a horizon he could not reach.

Sweetwater Walsh had been watching him speculatively. Now the grizzled little hostler said, "Seems like this feller Hubbard, that come here from the East, he don't much care if White Wolf is alive or dead, he's offerin' the reward all the same."

"Reward?" Crosswhite's belly knotted over the word, as if it were something rich and greasy and indigestible.

"Ain't that what I been tellin' you?"

"You didn't say anythin' about a reward."

"You ain't been listenin'. This feller Hubbard is fixin' up an expedition, like I said, to find White Wolf, that the cavalry is supposed to have shot up. Don't know what he wants with a dead Injun, or even a live one, but this particular redskin is worth a lot to him. He's puttin' up five hundred dollars in gold to the man who can lead him to that savage."

For a long moment Crosswhite did not speak. The words kept pounding at him with a force that was almost painful. Maybe another time they wouldn't have hit him so hard. Maybe it was all that had happened to him lately, losing his wages after busting his ribs, being shooed off Wishbone's place like something grubby and dangerous, having the storm nipping at his heels before he reached Cheyenne.

And most of all having Annie Macauley turn on him the way she did.

He wouldn't have to sell his saddle, he thought with leaping excitement.

Five hundred dollars!

And Lee Crosswhite was the only man who could lead this Easterner directly to White Wolf's grave. The only man alive.

17

Leland Resurrection Hubbard called himself an impresario of the unexpected, the daring, the different. He was first, last, and always a showman. What people wanted to see—even when they didn't yet know it themselves—he would bring before them. He had been a boy evangelist, following in the footsteps of his father, but in time he had yearned for more exotic and more exciting offerings—which, not incidentally, proved also to be more rewarding financially. All the way from mysterious India he had brought a giant elephant to astound the multitudes, who had paid eagerly for the privilege of viewing this great behemoth. He had staged traveling circuses and exhibited freaks of nature, from two-headed creatures pickled in jars to grotesque distortions of humanity. And in his most recent triumphs he had shipped buffalo from the plains of the Far West to stage an impressive "buffalo hunt" in sawdust rings in New York City and Boston and even in the nation's capital, complete with savage, painted Indians on their ponies and heroic buckskin-clad scouts circling the ring in pursuit, while the savages whooped and the guns of their pursuers crackled over the heads of the shaggy beasts of the Great Plains.

And now he had once again come to the West in search of what would be his greatest triumph.

"That is what I don't quite understand, sir," the polite young cavalry captain said.

"Understand?" Leland Hubbard smiled indulgently. "I would not expect you to understand, Captain. If all men saw the things I see, I would hardly be a successful entrepreneur, would I?"

"Well, I suppose not. But—"

"Yet it is only a matter of understanding human nature, Captain. If I am indeed successful at all, sir, it is in that understanding and perception."

"I see."

"I have the fullest authorization for this expedition, sir," Hubbard declared, a ring of authority in his tone. "If you would care to question that—"

"Not at all," the smooth-cheeked officer put in quickly. "General Bradley's compliments, Mr. Hubbard. He wished to be remembered to you. And I am directed to accompany and assist you in every way possible." He paused. "I was selected because I had the very good fortune to lead the detachment that intercepted White Wolf's party on the plains."

Hubbard was instantly more attentive. "For that I congratulate you, Captain. You have rendered this nation a great service. By heaven, it's a pleasure to meet you, sir. Would you mind telling me your name again?" Hubbard produced a note pad with a flourish, looked around, and snapped his fingers. Almost instantly a very tiny man appeared, a dwarf, with a portable ink case and a quill pen.

"Austin, sir. Arthur Austin."

"Then you know where this savage was last seen," Hubbard said as he wrote. "What extraordinary luck! I hadn't dared to hope to have you join my expedition, Captain. This is excellent news. You can lead us directly to White Wolf's whereabouts."

The officer regarded Leland Hubbard without expression. It was not clear whether he approved or disapproved of what he saw—or took any personal stand whatever. But—like virtually everyone in the Pike's Hotel Saloon—he could not deny the interest and fascination that Hubbard evoked.

Physically Leland Hubbard was a striking figure. He was probably in his fifties, with flowing white mustaches and long white hair that tended toward curls at the base of his neck. His complexion was colorfully florid but not unhealthy. He was not an exceptionally big man, but he had bulk—including an impressively large and solid stomach—and presence. His clothes, from his highly polished shoes to the tails of his black coat, were elegantly cut and fitted. The greatcoat he had worn when he entered the hotel lobby was adorned with a huge black beaver collar. His mustache curved in an upward sweep to match the line of his lips, pursed in a perpetual smile, as if he were greatly satisfied with life and his place in it. Austin had known such men in the past, including a cousin of his father's who had been in the Maryland legislature, and he knew better than to be earned along on the sweep of their words.

Nevertheless, Leland Resurrection Hubbard had influence in Washington, including powerful friends in the Department of the Army. General Bradley, whose command guarded the line of the Niobrara River, was not in the habit of sending detachments of cavalry to the aid of every civilian who came up with a scheme for an expedition into hostile territory. His orders to Austin had been explicit and unequivocal. Austin was to escort Hubbard's group and help him to accomplish his purpose. What remained unclear in Austin's mind was exactly what that purpose was. Hubbard had a way of talking in resounding generalities that left many questions unanswered.

He wanted White Wolf's body, that was clear enough. And, Austin thought with a certain cynicism, there would be profit in it for Leland Hubbard.

"Actually that may not be as easy as you might think, Mr. Hubbard," Austin said in belated reply. "I must tell you that we searched at some pains for Chief White Wolf after he escaped us, but without success. He knows those mountains far better than we do. And now, with the latest storm to cover any tracks—"

"But he was on foot, sir!"

"That's correct."

"And I am given to understand that he was wounded by the fire of your soldiers."

"Yes, sir. We are quite sure he was struck at least once." Leland Hubbard stabbed his long black cigar toward Austin in a triumphant flourish. "Then he cannot have got far, Captain! We are certain to find him. I understand that you could not pursue your search of one Indian when you were in the field, Captain—no apologies are necessary. But we will be under no such handicaps of duty on my expedition."

Austin smiled faintly. He wondered why Hubbard should have expected him to apologize. That was a way such men had of taking you down a peg, he thought, putting you in an inferior and defensive position.

Aloud he said, "It's possible that we may be faced with similar duties, Mr. Hubbard. I must warn you that there is a strong possibility that some of White Wolf's hotheaded followers may attempt to retaliate against any force put in their way. General Bradley is convinced that it would be unwise for your expedition to venture into unprotected terrain without a military escort."

Hubbard smiled broadly. "But that is why you are here, Captain, is it not?"

126

"Yes, sir."

"Do you think it's possible that White Wolf is still alive, and that he might have rejoined his band of savages?"

"It's . . . possible, Mr. Hubbard."

"You don't sound as if you believe it likely."

"Frankly, I don't, sir. For what it's worth, I don't think he could have got out of those mountains alive. But—"

"Out with it, Captain. What's on your mind?"

"Our soldiers had a far better chance of following him than any large expedition of civilians, Mr. Hubbard. And we had better weather. Now it's almost certain that severe storms may be expected at any time. What you propose is a journey with considerable risk and very little chance of success."

Hubbard smiled tolerantly. "Well, you have had your say, Captain. I can assure you that I am no stranger to hazard."

"Mr. Hubbard, I didn't mean to imply—"

"No offense taken, Captain Austin." Hubbard paused to puff on the black cigar and blow out a satisfied plume of smoke. "I believe you have left out one factor in our favor, and it is one that should not be underestimated."

"What is that, Mr. Hubbard?"

"Greed, Captain. I have offered a reward of five hundred dollars in gold to any man who can lead us to White Wolf."

"It seems unlikely—"

"On the contrary, Captain. I have already interviewed three men who claim on their honor to have personal knowledge of this savage's grave."

"*Three* men, sir?"

Hubbard smiled. "That is correct."

"With certain knowledge of three different graves, Mr. Hubbard?"

The impresario roared with laughter. "You are quite right, Captain Austin. The world is full of charlatans and thieves and liars. But who knows? We may yet find the man who is not lying. And when we do—" The tip of his cigar flared into bright red ash. "When we do, Captain, I assure you the world itself will take notice!"

18

Lee Crosswhite watched the white-haired entrepreneur and the young cavalry officer from across the hotel saloon. It was a large room, richly paneled in dark woods and hung with red velvet to frame the windows. There were handsome paintings in huge gilt frames on the walls and behind the long mahogany bar. At one end was a billiard table with a pair of lamps suspended above it. Crosswhite felt uncomfortable in these elegant surroundings, conscious of his worn clothes and empty pockets. He had saved enough—and that from Annie Macauley's money—for one drink. The glass with which he made circles on the bar had long been empty.

The captain rose and took his leave. Leland Hubbard leaned back expansively. After a moment he drew another cigar from a silver case and carefully severed its tip with a small cutting instrument designed for the purpose.

Crosswhite pushed away from the bar and crossed the room quickly. The flow of visitors to Hubbard's table had been steady, leaving little room for him to squeeze in.

"Mr. Hubbard?"

"You have the advantage of me, sir."

"Name's Crosswhite." He plunged straight

to the point. "I understand you have posted a reward."

Hubbard smiled. "I have, sir. Am I to take it that you are prepared to claim it?"

"Could be. If it's true you're puttin' up that gold for the man who can take you to White Wolf of the Lakotas."

"It seems that Indian was a man even more remarkable than his reputation as a warrior would suggest," Hubbard declared. "He seems to have been a man of many lives, and as many deaths as the proverbial cat."

"Wouldn't know about that," Crosswhite said, frowning.

Something in the seriousness of his manner caused Leland Hubbard to regard him more closely, dropping his bantering tone. "Sit down, Mr. Crosswhite. I am not having fun with you, be assured. It is just that you are the fourth man in twenty-four hours who has been ready to claim that reward. Can I buy you a drink, Mr. Crosswhite?"

Crosswhite shook his head, but he eased into the offered chair facing the Easterner.

"Nonsense," Hubbard insisted. "We'll have a drink, and then it will be time to adjourn to the dining room for a midday repast. You'll be good enough to join me there, Mr. Crosswhite?"

Reluctant to accept either food or drink, Crosswhite was also determined not to back off now, no matter how many men claimed to have buried White Wolf.

Somewhat more than an hour later, feeling stuffed and warm and grateful, he accepted a cigar from Leland Hubbard to smoke over a cup of rich, black coffee. Without question, he concluded, it was the finest cigar—and the finest meal—he had ever enjoyed.

"You say this Indian called himself White Wolf," Leland Hubbard said after several minutes' silence.

"Didn't exactly say that. What I said was he called out that name, clear as I'd speak my own." Crosswhite had an uneasy sense of weighting his words with special meaning. But he hadn't lied, he thought defensively; there was no longer any doubt in his mind about the identity of the old Indian.

Hubbard studied him across the table through their mutual smoke signals. "By God, sir, I believe you are telling me the truth!"

Crosswhite said nothing, thinking of the three hungry men who had told their stories before him.

"Your story rings true," Hubbard said. "You strike me as an honest man, Mr. Crosswhite, and I'm not sure I could say that about the other claimants."

Crosswhite was not sure how to reply to this either. It was not the kind of thing one man was accustomed to say to another in this part of the country. You assumed a man was honest unless he showed you otherwise. And if you were prepared to call him a liar, you had better be prepared also to back up that charge with fists or knife or gun.

"What makes you so certain of me?" he asked finally.

"I'm seldom wrong about people," Hubbard stated flatly, with the assurance of a man who seldom admitted himself wrong about anything. "And you were most emphatic about your Indian having been shot in the back. That is an important detail, Mr. Crosswhite—more important than you may have guessed. You're the only one to make such a claim, and you couldn't know it unless you really did treat White Wolf as you have said."

"It's true enough," Crosswhite agreed. "But I don't see how that proves anythin'."

"But it does, Mr. Crosswhite. It makes me quite convinced that you are the man I've been waiting for. I have the word of Captain Arthur Austin of the U. S. Cavalry that White Wolf was indeed shot in the back after bursting through the captain's lines. That specific fact has never been published to my certain knowledge. It was only said that White Wolf had been wounded but never exactly *how* he was injured."

So that was who the young officer was, Crosswhite thought. He had not anticipated anyone doubting his story, but he hadn't expected others to come forward with rival claims. It was clear that he was fortunate to have Austin on hand.

Maybe his luck was turning right around.

"I'll want you to have a talk with Captain Austin," Hubbard said with visibly rising enthusiasm. "We'll want to start our expedition as soon as possible. And this can be only the beginning of our endeavors together, Mr. Crosswhite. You'll not regret this day, I assure you." For some time Hubbard had been examining this lean-faced cowhand appraisingly, sizing up his tall figure and his angular, almost gaunt features, picturing to what use that image might be turned. "This can be the beginning of great ventures for you, and I don't mean only that reward. Do you understand what I intend to do, Mr. Crosswhite?"

"I was sorta wonderin' about that. Seems like a lot of trouble and expense to go to over an Indian, even a warrior like White Wolf."

"That's because you're a Westerner, Mr. Crosswhite," Hubbard answered. "Indians are a familiar sight to you. Perhaps you have fought them, killed them, seen examples of their savage lust."

"Well, I wouldn't say—"

"You cannot understand the fearful curiosity of the Easterner who has never seen a painted Plains Indian in the flesh. And especially one as renowned as White Wolf. I tell you, Mr.

Crosswhite, if you can lead me to that great warrior's grave, if he is dead, or to the man himself if he is alive, I'll make you as famous as Buffalo Bill himself!"

Crosswhite stared at him. "Well, I don't know . . . What is it you have in mind, Mr. Hubbard?"

"Look around you, sir. Consider the repast you have enjoyed during this past hour. Fine food and drink, a good cigar—these are only small things. There is a great world out there to the east that I don't think it presumptuous to suggest you have never dreamed of. What is your fancy, sir? Clothes? French brandy? Adoring women? Gambling? Racing superb horseflesh? I'm offering you that world, Mr. Crosswhite!"

"Well, uh, that reward would be enough—"

"Oh, you shall have your gold, Mr. Crosswhite. And more where it came from. You just take me to White Wolf, that's all. Leave the rest to me. I like you, sir. In the right clothes and sitting a fine horse—yes, sir, I like what I see."

Crosswhite sat bemused. The picture Leland Hubbard sketched was both startling and awesome, but he could not really see himself in it. Yet he could not deny the satisfactions of sitting in this gracious dining room with its white-covered tables, gleaming silverware, and graceful glass and china against a background of smoothly polished woods, sitting back with his belly pleasurably full, a long cigar between his teeth, and a feeling of pampered ease stealing over him. Why not? Why should anything be beyond his reach? Hubbard was offering him another horizon, that was all, perhaps one more wonderful than any he had ever dreamed of reaching.

He wondered what Annie Macauley would have to say now.

Suddenly Leland Hubbard's attention shifted. He half rose from his chair. "Ah, here is one of your new colleagues, who has already seen fit to join our expedition. We do not go unprepared, Mr. Crosswhite, as you will see. This way, Mr. Rossiter. I believe I have found our man!"

Crosswhite stumbled to his feet, turning, his stomach twisting over its heavy meal.

He saw the white expanse of Sut Rossiter's smile before it froze.

Leland Hubbard's alert glance shifted between the two men. "You two men know each other?"

"We do," Crosswhite snapped. "I know him for a cheat and a liar."

"Here now, that is intemperate, sir. Surely—"

"Let him say what he has to say," Rossiter cut in. "A man's got a right to his last words."

"I've done my talking."

"Then you'll die in a warm room."

"One place is as good as another."

Crosswhite was backing slowly away from the table, facing Rossiter, putting a few more feet between them. The gambler was wearing a greatcoat, thick with sheep's wool. It would hinder him, Crosswhite thought, judging his chances. Rossiter seemed contemptuously confident. He had shoved the flap of his coat aside, exposing one of his white-handled guns.

Crosswhite wished he hadn't eaten and drunk so heartily, but he had been waiting too long for this meeting to regret it now.

There had been a stir of excitement throughout the dining room, followed by the scuttle of hasty movement. Crosswhite did not take his eyes from Rossiter's face.

Suddenly Leland Hubbard was between them, glaring from one man to the other, his initial astonishment replaced by outrage. "Hold on—I'll not have this!"

"It has nothin' to do with you," Crosswhite said.

"Do you think I have journeyed all this way across the prairie to have my plans thwarted by some quarrel? It has everything to do with me." He whirled to face Rossiter. "Cover your guns, Mr. Rossiter. I have hired them for my purpose. And for that I also need Mr. Crosswhite alive."

"That saddlebum? What use is he to you?"

"He buried White Wolf!" Hubbard thundered.

The ringing declaration brought an audible gasp from the safe corners of the saloon, followed by the buzz of excited talk. "He buried him, and he can lead us to that grave. This is worth far too much to all of us, sir, for me to let it be jeopardized now."

"You'd take his word?" Rossiter asked with a sneer. "He has lost his wages to me at cards, so it's my guess he's a hungry man who'd say anything for that reward you've posted."

"Do you think liars and connivers are strangers to me?" Hubbard demanded scornfully. "I know my man. Mr. Crosswhite has seen what he claims to have seen. I'll stake my entire expedition on that judgment. Hear his story and you'll agree with me, Mr. Rossiter."

"No man calls me a liar," Rossiter snapped. But he spoke less aggressively. His eyes shifted, weighing, worrying. Hubbard had surprising control over him, Crosswhite thought.

And over him as well? Was that why he had remained silent?

"Stand aside, Mr. Hubbard," Crosswhite said.

"No, sir. I care nothing for your differences with Mr. Rossiter. They are of no importance to me. If you wish to settle those differences in your own way when our expedition is successfully concluded, if you would risk all that I am prepared to discover to you, you may so choose. But I'll not stand aside now."

Crosswhite hesitated. The clash with Rossiter could never be forgotten. Could it be postponed? Was anything lost by that delay?

Seeing his hesitation, Leland Hubbard seized upon it shrewdly. "It's agreed then. Gentlemen, you will put up your guns and set aside your quarrel, whatever it might be, until our business is concluded. Otherwise there is no agreement between us for your services, Mr. Rossiter. And no reward, Mr. Crosswhite."

Was that it? Crosswhite asked himself. The promise of gold? Was that all that stayed his hatred? Did gold mean so much?

Rossiter was scowling but silent. What promises had Hubbard made him over full belly and fat cigar? Enough to purchase—what? His two guns?

Crosswhite felt angry with himself, but still he waited, his purpose blunted, even the diverting of his wrath from Rossiter to himself helping to change the thrust and heat of that rage.

Rossiter would not escape, he heard himself argue. And hearing that inner voice he knew that Leland Hubbard had won.

The impresario moved quickly to his side. "It's best if you withdraw, Mr. Crosswhite. I'll speak to Rossiter." He pressed something into Crosswhite's palm and folded his fingers over it. The clink and weight of coins filled the closed fist. "You'll want to prepare yourself, sir, for the journey. Think of your future, Mr. Crosswhite. Don't throw it all away!"

Then he turned away, and it was Rossiter's arm he was gripping with his smooth white fingers, Rossiter's ear he spoke into with soft urgency, Rossiter he steered toward his table.

A fuller swell of excited murmuring rose around them and Crosswhite, who stood as if forgotten and ignored, wavering, one part of him wanting to call the moment back, the other insisting that he could wait, that nothing was lost in the delay.

He turned aside, still angry, his fist closed over the uncounted coins Hubbard had given him. He left the dining room and stalked blindly through the hotel lobby. Outside the cold air made his skin tighten, and his eyes nearly closed against the glare of the sunlight off broad sheets of snow.

It didn't matter how insistently he argued with himself. There was a cold weight now replacing the satisfied fullness in his belly.

Something had been lost.

19

Annie Macauley did not conceal her surprise. "You met this Rossiter?"

"Yep."

"And you didn't . . . fight?"

Crosswhite shook his head.

She continued to stare at him. "I'm glad, Lee."

He grunted, wishing she would stop looking at him in that puzzled, speculative way. "It's what you wanted," he growled.

"Yes." For a moment she was silent. "I wanted you alive."

"It's only postponed," Crosswhite pointed out for the second time. "Don't know why this Hubbard thinks he has to have Rossiter's guns along on his expedition, when he has the cavalry to ride escort. But that ain't for me to decide. When it's over—" He shrugged.

"Maybe you'll change your mind again. I'm glad it's put off, anyway." But the odd look of surprise lingered in Annie's eyes. "Do you really know where this Indian can be found?"

"If he's where I left him. Course, it's possible some of his own kin might have found him 'fore this."

"Five hundred dollars." Her lips seemed to test

the hardness and value of the words. "It's a great deal of money."

Crosswhite grinned. "As much as you had in those two hats, I reckon, back in Denver."

"More," Annie said.

A silence fell between them. After a while Crosswhite shifted restlessly. The silence was not a comfortable one. Was she still angry with him over his abrupt proposal of marriage? He had felt better about accepting her offer of supper when he was able to come with coins to repay her loan, but had he made a mistake in returning so soon?

Finally he got it out. "Did you mean what you said this mornin'?"

"I did, Lee."

He was slow to answer. "Been a long time." How many winters had he headed this way, knowing the kind of welcome that would be waiting for him? How many long rides had been shortened by that prospect?

"Yes, a very long time." The words had been said only a few days before, but now they were heavy with sadness.

Maybe that was what was eating at her, he thought, those five years of waiting for him to say something he couldn't say. But why hadn't she kicked him out long before? Why wait until he *did* come out with the proposal she had yearned to hear, by her own admission? That didn't make sense.

Only a woman's kind of sense.

There had been other women during those years, maybe in a crib back of a mining camp or in one of the elegant houses in Helena, but none of them had mattered. He couldn't remember any names or faces. Annie Macauley was the only one who counted as more than a moment's pleasure or release. Hell's fire, didn't she know that?

He wondered if there had been other men for her during those years since Denver. There had been long spells, six months and more between his visits to Cheyenne City. He could hardly blame her if there had been others, although the thought made him squirm restlessly on the hard wooden chair in Annie's kitchen. And if there had been, well, they were faceless men to her like his crib women, he was sure of that.

Suddenly he knew that there had been no one, leastwise not for many years, not since they had become close. He couldn't ask her—not at this moment, the way she was feeling—but he was sure.

He had kept telling himself that she would calm down after a while, but he saw no yielding in her eyes or mouth now, no sympathy or softness.

Just that puzzled question over his run-in with Sut Rossiter.

"It's changed between us." The words came hard.

"Yes."

"It don't have to be."

"You did that, Lee."

He wondered how far he should push her. Had everything already been lost?

No. Come back in the spring, she had said, and ask me that same question. Then I'll believe you mean it.

Spring seemed a long way off.

The silence in the kitchen ticked slowly with the beat of the clock. It was heavy and sad, and Crosswhite wished that he could do something to change it, but this was not the time.

"That reward means a lot to you," Annie Macauley said at last, and it seemed to him that she was deliberately changing the subject, turning away from any more talk about *them* toward safer subjects.

He was wrong again, as he quickly learned. The reward was not a safe topic.

"A man don't like to cadge drinks all the time, or eat on credit." Or be turned out into the cold by his woman.

"I hope it's worth it to you. It just—"

"What are you gettin' at?"

"It's not like you, Lee."

"Seems like everythin' I do is all wrong all of a sudden."

"That's not true. But you buried that old Indian, Lee. You put him where you did because you thought it was right, that he had that much coming to him, just being a brave man. That's what you said."

"He's only a savage," Crosswhite growled.

"Do you honestly believe that? Is that why you nursed him after he tried to steal your horse and kill you?"

"You're tryin' to turn my own words against me."

"It's not hard," she said in a strange, cold way. In that moment he found it difficult to find in this stranger across the table the warm, loving woman who had greeted him on his return to Cheyenne City, a snowman coming out of the darkness to stamp his cold boots on her doorstep.

"I reckon there ain't no use in us talkin'."

"It seems that way."

Crosswhite rose. The chair scraped loudly. The light from the kerosene lamp threw his shadow against the wall behind him, a giant's shadow that covered the wall and spilled across the ceiling. "Maybe I won't be back," he said.

"Oh, God! Just go! Don't say things like that to make me feel sorry for you or for myself. Go on! Go to your Mr. Hubbard and let him turn you into a circus cowboy if that's what you want."

"I'm goin'." He stalked through the house to the front door, each thump of boot an emphatic warning that she had gone too far.

"Just do one thing for me, Lee," she called after him, stopping him at the door. He held it closed against the sharp wedge of cold that tried to get in. "Just for my curiosity, ask your Mr. Hubbard what he wants White Wolf for. What does he mean to do with an old Indian who is dead and can't bring harm to anyone any more? Do you know, Lee Crosswhite? Or were your eyes too busy shining over that gold you are going to win?"

He whirled. "I don't know, and it's no matter to me what he does. That Indian's dead, and it can't hurt him none either. Seems to me you didn't used to be so particular about a hatful of money and where it came from."

Even across the room in the pale yellow light he saw the quick start of tears in her eyes. He took a step away from the door, wanting to pull back his last words.

"No, don't," she whispered. "I'll hear no more."

"Annie—"

"Goodbye, Lee. I hope you get what you want. Just go."

She wasn't even looking at him. She hugged her body with her arms as if she was cold, and leaned sideways, turning slightly to rest her head against the frame of the kitchen door.

20

Crosswhite had told Leland Hubbard that it was little more than a three- or four-day journey to the canyon mouth where he had left White Wolf's body. Near the end of the expedition's third day out of Cheyenne City he realized that he had miscalculated.

The snowdrifts were one reason. Leaving Cheyenne City the company had enjoyed clear skies, but the sun was pale and lacked the warmth necessary to melt the deep snows from recent storms. The air remained sharply cold.

At least the Indian chief's body should be in acceptable condition, Hubbard said in commenting over the weather. It had been freezing cold every day since Crosswhite had buried him in the tree. "That's important to us, Mr. Crosswhite," he said. "This cold is a blessing."

"Let's hope the wolves haven't got at him," Crosswhite answered. Reluctantly he remembered Annie Macauley's taunting question: What did Hubbard want with a dead Indian?

He said nothing then. There had to be a good reason.

In addition to the deep snow that covered tracks and forced the caravan to pick its way often over unmarked terrain, or to find new paths when old ones disappeared, the very size of the train slowed it down. Crosswhite had been alone, his two horses lightly laden when he came this way. Leland Resurrection Hubbard did nothing in so casual a fashion. Besides Captain Austin's detachment of cavalry—numbering about thirty men in Crosswhite's quick tally, counting Austin and his junior officer, Lieutenant Schaefer— Hubbard had assembled four wagons and nearly a score of men. The wagons were lumbering and slow compared to men on horseback. The wagon drivers had to stay on established trails to cover any ground at reasonable speed, and to choose the easiest routes when there were no beaten paths showing. The crew was slow to pull itself together in the morning—Hubbard, for instance, insisted on washing his long hair and trimming his flowing white mustache and beard each day— and quick to search for a pleasant campsite while light still held. And dark came early on these short winter days.

For that nightly camp the ground had to be cleared to make space for Hubbard's large tent. He slept on a raised cot inside the tent's shelter. A work table or desk was opened out and set up each night under roof, and Hubbard would sit at the table for some time after dark, a lamp resting on the work surface and throwing its yellow light through the front flaps across the trampled snow outside. He was like an army commander in the field preparing for the next day's assault. By contrast Captain Austin, though he also traveled with a tent, cared little for his comfort and traveled lightly and efficiently.

Meals were elaborate. One heavy wagon seemed to carry nothing but tins of fruit and vegetables, sardines, fresh and dried meats, nuts and cheeses and assorted breads, and some other delicacies that were strange to Crosswhite. Hubbard even had assorted jams to spread on his morning biscuits. Leland Hubbard considered himself an explorer into the hostile mysteries of the West and its Great Plains, but he had come with as many of the trappings and pleasures of eastern civilization as his expedition could carry.

Sut Rossiter seemed to have taken an important place in that company. He rode at Hubbard's side much of each day, the two conversing often. He retired with Hubbard into the entrepreneur's tent in the evenings, sharing Hubbard's meals, which were individually prepared for them by a gnarled stump of a man named Vorec, whom Crosswhite had first noticed at the hotel bringing Hubbard his pen and ink. Vorec—"my man," as Hubbard called him—looked as if his legs had been cut off at the knees. He stood hardly more than half the height of an average man. He was a taciturn, dour-looking man with a rasping voice. He seemed intensely loyal to Leland Hubbard, and—

judging by the smells that came from Hubbard's tent at mealtimes—he was an excellent cook.

Rossiter made a point of joking with the dwarf often. Although Vorec did not seem particularly responsive, Hubbard seemed pleased.

Every crew had a man like Rossiter, Crosswhite thought sourly. He was the man who could always sniff out an easier task, who kept busier buttering up the strawboss than he ever did with a branding iron or a rope. The only thing different about Sut Rossiter was that he was as dangerous as a copperhead fighting for raft space in a flood.

Rossiter was in Leland Hubbard's tent when the leader of the caravan summoned Crosswhite after supper on the third night out of Cheyenne. The big gambler seemed outsize for even so large a tent. Hatless, he still had to stoop and bend his neck when he moved to sit on a large chest behind Hubbard's desk. As Crosswhite entered, Vorec, who had brought Hubbard's message, left the tent, but Crosswhite sensed that he never went far, that he was always hovering just outside the flaps in the event that Hubbard should call. And did he carry a vest-pocket gun to suit his size, a derringer or Remington hidden under his coat or in a concealed wrist-holster? It would be like Hubbard to have such a bodyguard. But what did it take to inspire the fierce loyalty he saw in Vorec? More than gold, he thought.

"Ah, Mr. Crosswhite! You should have joined

us earlier for supper—an oversight on my part, sir, unintentional, I assure you."

"Company grub's fine."

"Good, good." Leland Hubbard paused to light one of his ever-present cigars. "Captain Austin will be with us shortly. Ah, Captain—come in, come in. Good of you and Mr. Crosswhite to join us."

"Not at all, sir." Austin nodded to Rossiter and Lee Crosswhite, who had several times discussed his run-in with White Wolf and his trail from there to Cheyenne City with the young officer. He liked Austin, who seemed sensible and unimpressed with his own rank, but at the same time capable of exercising a quiet leadership of his men.

"Can I offer you a brandy, gentlemen? No? Let's get right down to business then," Hubbard said. "Mr. Crosswhite, how long did you say you rode from that canyon where you encountered White Wolf?"

"To Cheyenne City? Three days." Crosswhite considered, although he had been over this with Hubbard before as well as Austin. "I wasn't ridin' hard, and I didn't start early that day I put him in the tree. Lost half the day, I'd guess. A man on horseback in a hurry, he could have done it easy in two days, especially if he was willin' to take some dark."

Hubbard nodded, savoring his cigar. Smoke

already filled the tent. "We have been three days on the trail," he pointed out.

Crosswhite nodded. "It's slower with wagons, and there's more snow. We camped last night on the south fork of Horse Creek after two full days. I rode that distance in one."

"Huh!" Rossiter snorted in derision. "Are you still gonna listen to him, Mr. Hubbard? I told you before we ever left Cheyenne, he never seen White Wolf, dead or alive. His whole story has a high smell."

Crosswhite felt the flush of anger hot on his neck. Hubbard saw it and spoke quickly, heading off his retort. "That is hardly reasonable, Mr. Rossiter."

"A man will do unreasonable things for gold, especially a drifter who's come up empty."

"I must point out in all fairness that Mr. Crosswhite has neither asked for nor received that reward. This line of discussion is of no advantage to us, Rossiter. It was agreed that any differences between you two would be postponed until our expedition returns to Cheyenne City."

"I didn't exactly bargain for that," Rossiter answered.

Hubbard spun away from his desk. "I have your word—"

"Only that he'd stay alive long enough to take you to that Indian. That's all."

The words lingered in the taut silence that

followed inside the tent. They told Crosswhite what he had not needed to hear: Any truce between him and Rossiter ended the moment White Wolf's elevated grave was discovered.

"Very well then," Hubbard said testily. "I'll hear no more about it. The fact is that both Captain Austin and myself have heard Mr. Crosswhite's story and accept its authenticity. His description of White Wolf is quite accurate, and the details of his wound and his circumstances corroborate other facts previously known only to Captain Austin. Is that not correct, Captain?"

"Yes, sir." The cavalryman had observed the exchange between Rossiter and Crosswhite in silence but with alert interest. He would judge it, Crosswhite thought, for any risk it might present to Austin's command.

"Very well then." If this dismissal of Rossiter's interruption disturbed the big man, he did not show it. He stared at Crosswhite contemptuously past the white-haired impresario's shoulder, his rows of big white teeth revealed in a faintly mocking smile. "What I wish to know now, Mr. Crosswhite, is how close we are to that canyon you mentioned."

It had been a peculiar exchange, Crosswhite thought, working over old ground, establishing an animosity between him and Rossiter that had long ago been established—unless the whole quarrel had been restaged deliberately in front of

Captain Austin, But that suggested that Hubbard and Rossiter were working in harness together in ways Crosswhite did not yet understand.

He shrugged. "Like I told you, we're not covering half the distance in a day that a man rides with nothin' to slow him down. If I was to guess I'd say it'll take us one more day pullin' north to find Chugwater Creek. From there it's another day, goin' west, to that little creek where I camped. It spills right out of the hills. That's two more days to travel, unless you want to leave these wagons behind."

Hubbard hesitated. "I can't do that."

"Might take us even longer when we get into them foothills," Crosswhite said. "There's one draw I recollect that's easy enough for a man on a horse. It'll take some crossin' with wagons."

"We'll be climbing, sir?"

"Some."

Leland Hubbard frowned. This territory was romantic in the stories told about it, picturesque when viewed from the windows of a train speeding across the prairie, wildly beautiful on the artist's canvas, but the hard fact of it was somewhat different. Its vastness threatened to shrink a man's vision of himself. Hubbard had never found a door he could not talk his way through, nor an obstacle he could not surmount by perseverance or cunning. These high plains and mountains threatened him in a way he had never before experienced. Its chasms were deeper, its peaks higher, its cold winds sweeping down the flanks of the mountains more threatening than any he had known. You could believe those winds might come howling like something alive, with a force no man could stand against.

These emotions were new to Leland Hubbard, and they disturbed him more than he cared to admit. He did not relish the prospect of an arduous climb through deepening snows or the threat of unknown chasms.

Now he reminded himself that the prize was worth the hazard. Nothing of great value was ever won without cost or risk.

"What about the weather? My man Vorec insists that it will take a turn for the worse, that a storm is coming. His bones tell him so." Hubbard smiled, as if he were not sure of the value of bones in predicting weather. "What do you think, Crosswhite?"

"He could be right. This time of year it can change awful sudden. If it does—" He shrugged once more. If a real storm struck they would never find White Wolf, not before spring. He saw no gain in adding that they might also find themselves dangerously isolated.

Hubbard sighed. "We'll take the wagons with us another day," he decided. "We should camp tomorrow night on that creek you mentioned. There'll be shelter there?"

Crosswhite nodded.

"Then, if you can assure me we're close to our goal, Mr. Crosswhite, we'll ride on ahead without the wagons to hold us back. We should be able to reach our destination and return to the wagons on the same day. That will save us considerable time. Do you agree, Mr. Rossiter?"

Rossiter shrugged massively. "It's your deal, Mr. Hubbard."

"I take it Mr. Crosswhite will also agree, since I'm following your suggestion about the wagons, at least halfway. And you, Captain Austin?"

"My orders, as you know, are to accompany and assist, and I see no reason to question them now. The Army is also anxious to verify the fact of White Wolf's death, sir—although Mr. Crosswhite's testimony leaves little doubt. Your plan seems sound enough, Mr. Hubbard."

"Good, good. This is a worthy venture, gentlemen, and I assure you it is one your countrymen will not soon forget!"

21

Draws-Out-Arrows knew that his brother had gone to find his welcome among the tipis of his ancestors. One of the braves who had followed White Wolf on the hunt, and been caught in the pony soldiers' ambush, had returned to the field of battle after his initial flight, attempting to regain some honor by watching the bluecoats at a distance. Later that day he had seen White Wolf's favorite horse, riderless, walking with those of the white soldiers.

White Wolf had been surprised by the enemy. This fact was remarkable to Draws-Out-Arrows, but there were many mysteries in life to which no clear answers were given.

Now Draws-Out-Arrows spoke to the survivors of the fallen leader's village. It had snowed briefly during the night, and the air was very cold. He had to squint against the sun glitter off the fresh snow. Small puffs of mist accompanied his words as they broke from his lips. The painted robe he wore around his shoulders was hairless, but he was indifferent to the teeth of the wind.

Draws-Out-Arrows had not accompanied his brother White Wolf on the last hunt. He spoke this truth sorrowfully, for it would have been good to die in battle at his great brother's side, fighting the hated pony soldiers.

Draws-Out-Arrows was ten winters younger than White Wolf. He was a fighting man still in his prime, and he had gladly joined his brother in defiance of the white man's demands that they submit meekly like toothless old women to the humiliations heaped upon them in the name of peace. The white man's promises were less enduring than the white flakes that fell from the sky. The only certainty about the white man was his treachery.

As a youth, Draws-Out-Arrows had been renamed by his parents for the skill and bravery he had shown in battle against the enemies of his people, specifically for that horseman's skill of hanging behind the body of his running pony by a single leg and hand even at full gallop, drawing the harmless arrows of his foes while presenting no real target. He had borne his new name with pride. In the years of his manhood Draws-Out-Arrows had counted many coups. He wore in his hair the feathers of the golden eagle. Upon his lance hung the scalps of many enemies he had slain.

He did not grieve for his fallen brother. No, he envied him. Draws-Out-Arrows could ask for no greater glory than to die on that same field of battle where White Wolf had fallen, against those same enemies.

The warrior paused, glaring fiercely at the circle of warriors gathered before the tipi and at the outer ring of women and children who listened to his words. In boasting of past valor and future vengeance, Draws-Out-Arrows did not speak idly. He honored both himself and his brother.

"It is the duty of the family to avenge our brother," Draws-Out-Arrows said then. "I pledge that vengeance upon the *wasicu.* I promise all my brothers that a scalp will be taken from the head of a great white war leader, one as famed among his people as White Wolf was honored among the Lakotas. I pledge this trophy myself, for only thus will our brother White Wolf return to dwell among us!"

The scalp that Draws-Out-Arrows thus publicly pledged would be the symbol of his lost brother's spirit. Like all of his people, Draws-Out-Arrows believed that the human spirit was somehow directly associated with human hair. The scalp he would take would be more than a bloody badge of victory. It would be the way in which White Wolf would be enabled to return to his village, mysteriously reborn in the form of the scalp torn from his enemy.

Draws-Out-Arrows told the assembled warriors that he and his brothers and cousins gladly accepted the honor and duty of this act of vengeance. But he also invited all of his brothers of the Lakotas, the Teton Sioux, all who had proudly followed White Wolf's lance into battle, to join him now in a ceremony of death. By this would they swear to join him also in avenging White Wolf by counting coup over the bodies of the great leader's enemies, and by the taking of the white leader's scalp.

When he had finished, Draws-Out-Arrows turned and withdrew into his family tipi. He took his place on the far side, sitting on a blanket and facing the entry. To one side were White Wolf's wife and the wife of Draws-Out-Arrows, along with her sister and other female relatives. One by one the male warriors entered, relatives and followers alike. While the men watched stoically, each of the women, many of them keening and crying piteously, slashed their thighs three times with the ceremonial knife, passing it along from one to the other. When all had drawn blood, the knife passed among them once more, this time used by each woman to cut her hair short.

Now it was the turn of the men, who sat in a crowded circle that was in many places two-deep, so many had come into the tipi in response to Draws-Out-Arrows' invitation. He moved slowly around the circle, pausing before each brave warrior to insert finely sharpened wooden pegs through his skin, three pegs in the leg and two in the arm of each man. Then he returned to his own place. Wounded Heel, a cousin, had the honor of drawing the five sharpened pegs through the pinched skin of Draws-Out-Arrows, who endured the ordeal without so much as a grimace. When this was done the men, like the women, cut their hair short in White Wolf's honor.

The first phase of the ceremony of death was complete. The hair each man and woman present at the ceremony had lost would grow back, but the small, self-inflicted wounds would heal into scars that each would carry in White Wolf's memory all the days of their lives.

While these acts of mourning were taking place, others of White Wolf's family were busy outside the tipi, erecting a simple, free-standing scaffold on the level plateau below the lodges. The women peeled the bark from the forked posts of the scaffold and painted black bands upon them to memorialize each of the coups White Wolf had won in his lifetime. The frame supported by these posts would have held the warrior's body if he had been brought back to the village. Now it would carry the badges and symbols of what he had been: the weapons he had not carried with him on the hunt, including his decorated lance; the makeup kit of war paint he had not believed it necessary to take along on the hunt; his flute; the spirit moccasins with their beaded soles, which were not made to be worn upon the earth but only along the Trail of Spirits; the war trophies he had won; his feathered war bonnet in its rawhide case; and last, the painted buffalo robe he had left behind in his tipi.

Draws-Out-Arrows now led the group of mourners from his tipi. He had asked that all of his horses, and all those of White Wolf except for the favorite he had ridden on the hunt, be brought before the tipi. Now, one by one, Draws-Out-Arrows gave away the ponies—his most valued possessions—to the assembled warriors. He kept only one horse, the one he would soon ride into battle.

The keening of the women was louder. On the plateau below the village, visible from where Draws-Out-Arrows now stood, a tipi was being raised over the memorial scaffold. It was unadorned, unpainted, so that no enemy would know who slept within. The snow having been brushed away by hand, the edges of the tipi were picketed tightly. The door and the smoke flaps were sewn tight.

This was White Wolf's spirit lodge. It would stand unmolested until the skins of the tipi aged and crumbled and withered away, and the winds pulled down the dried branches of the scaffold and the last remnants of the great warrior's belongings were scattered across the plain. In building it, as in the formal burial ceremony conducted without the body of the dead man, the Sioux paid their highest tribute to one of their leaders.

The ceremony had reached its climax. Wounded Heel received the honor of drawing the pegs with which each man had voluntarily been impaled. In the background the grieving women moaned like the wind, but none of the warriors made a sound as Wounded Heel moved from one to another. All of the bloody pegs were placed in a single pile. Drops of blood spotted the snow with the brilliant red of warpaint.

Now Draws-Out-Arrows, closest of White Wolf's relatives, took the knife that the women had used within the tipi to make shallow slashes across their legs. He handed the knife to Wounded Heel. Holding out his left arm, Draws-Out-Arrows pinched a fold of flesh away from the arm. At his grim nod Wounded Heel thrust the point of the knife through the raised layer of skin. "The brave White Wolf," Draws-Out-Arrows sang out, "leader of the Lakotas, did not come back."

The knife was passed to each warrior, each requesting his neighbor to thrust it through a fold of flesh in his arm, and as each received the wound he sang, "The brave White Wolf did not return."

It was over. There remained only the feast that Draws-Out-Arrows, according to the custom, had ordered prepared by the women of the family for all those who had joined in the mourning.

He himself was not hungry. His ceremonial

duties completed, he felt a renewal of the sadness that had been put off with conscious effort, and that he recognized as being unbefitting a warrior of his tribe, brother to White Wolf. While the food was being passed among the braves who would soon ride with him into battle, Draws-Out-Arrows withdrew alone from the area of the festivities. His moccasined feet made soundless tracks across the fresh snow.

At the edge of the group of lodges he paused, looking down at the lone *tiokete* on the plateau below, White Wolf's spirit lodge.

"Soon I will be with you, my brother," Draws-Out-Arrows said aloud. "We will hunt together once more in the land where there are always buffalo to be found nearby. But before I come I will do this thing. The Moon of the Long Days is near, but nothing will hold us back, not the sore eyes that come with the glaring snows, not the might of the pony soldiers, not the absence of the buffalo and the elk, and bellies that make thunder. We will ride against the enemies you have shown us how to fight, and we will not be afraid."

For a moment he paused, stirred by the passion of his own words and by the proud memories they evoked. Then he said, "Skan, the sky, will judge us. I will welcome that judgment, for you will be avenged, my brother. The scalp of a white leader will bring your spirit back to us.

"This is what Draws-Out-Arrows pledges."

He was silent. Around him the wind stirred the light top coating of snow into fine currents and drifts. Draws-Out-Arrows listened closely to the voice of the wind. At last he heard a sigh, a soft breath such as a man makes when he would nod his head in agreement. Draws-Out-Arrows felt the wind all around him then, around him and in him, and he knew that he was right in making his promise.

The wind blew cold against his eyes, drawing tears, and he knew that this was another sign.

22

The tracks of the buffalo herd were clear in the new snow. Clear and fresh.

"How old, do you think, Mr. Crosswhite?" Leland Hubbard asked jovially. Crosswhite was riding at the point of the caravan in between two of Captain Austin's soldiers who were assigned as flankers.

"I reckon they just beat us across this flat."

"Is that so? By Jove!" Excitement flashed in Leland Hubbard's bright blue eyes. "Splendid! I hadn't counted on a buffalo hunt for this expedition."

"You gonna take time for that?"

"If the tracks are as recent as you say, they can't be far. Surely it won't delay us for long."

Crosswhite grunted noncommittally. Everything Hubbard did seemed to take a little longer than expected, because it had to be done with a flourish. However, it wouldn't take long to track down the small herd, which appeared to be moving slowly south in search of grass. Crosswhite was a little surprised that they hadn't headed south before this, ahead of the worst winter storms. But some of the shaggy buffaloes had been known to survive winter on the high plains, somehow drifting away from the larger herds.

Crosswhite hadn't thought that the caravan was running short of meat already, but it was an oversize expedition for its purpose, and he supposed that the supplies would dwindle quickly. Fresh meat was always welcome.

The hunting expedition numbered half a dozen men in addition to Crosswhite: Leland Hubbard, Rossiter, Austin and Sergeant Jamison of the cavalry, the dwarf Vorec, and another of Hubbard's crew named Roget. The latter, Hubbard confided, had been with him on many a sporting hunt. He had the long-range squint and the silent ways of a hunter.

Vorec looked even smaller and out-of-place on his small piebald pony. Although the stirrups were raised as high as possible, he still had to stand straight up to reach them. Nevertheless, he handled the pony easily. His arms were almost as big around and as strong as a normal-size man's.

From the top of a rise the hunters spotted the herd of buffaloes—a drove numbering about thirty, moving slowly in their quest for grass under the snow. They were about two miles away. The wind was favorable, and Crosswhite judged that they should be able to ride close before any alarm was given.

"A splendid sight!" Hubbard exclaimed as the hunting party paused on the rise. "Though it's a small herd, isn't it? I remember Buffalo Bill Cody telling me of one occasion when he participated in a killing match and personally brought down more than sixty buffaloes in a single day's hunt! Sixty, gentlemen! Why, there are not more than half as many in that herd below us."

"Maybe that's why," Crosswhite said curtly. He was not sure why Hubbard's manner irritated him—why so many things had begun to rasp and rub him the wrong way on this excursion.

Hubbard turned a startled glance on him, then smiled broadly, taking Crosswhite's remark as a jest. "I should tell Bill Cody what you said when I next see him. A remarkable man, as you all must know, with whom I have had the pleasure of joining in profitable enterprise from time to time. This rifle"—he held out the long-barreled .50-caliber Springfield breechloader—"was a gift from Mr. Cody himself! One of his own buffalo hunting weapons. Perhaps even the very one that brought down those sixty buffaloes in a single day's hunt. I see you are carrying a Winchester, Mr. Crosswhite. You'll shoot more often than I, to be sure, but I'll warrant you'll not bring down more game than this rifle of mine."

"I wasn't figgerin' on any . . . killing match," Crosswhite said quietly.

The remark drew a slight smile from Captain Austin, but Hubbard did not notice.

"None proposed," Hubbard said good-naturedly. Nothing seemed able to ruffle his humor this morning. "Shall we close on them, gentlemen? Lead the way, Mr. Crosswhite!"

The wind held true, and there was a long dip that shut them off from the herd as they approached. When the shaggy beasts again came into view, they were less than five hundred yards away.

"I'll try to turn them in a circle," Crosswhite called out softly. "That'll give each man his animal, and save us all a long chase."

"Good God!" Leland Hubbard cried. "What is that?"

Crosswhite looked where Hubbard's arm pointed, toward another ridge downwind from the buffalo herd. A number of much smaller animals slunk restlessly across the rim of the ridge, back and forth, back and forth. They had spotted rival hunters, Crosswhite thought.

"Wolves," he said. "They're following the herd."

"Wolves!"

"They're hungry, too."

Hubbard stared across the long sweep of fresh snow that had fallen during the night, his eyes alight, his face red with the cold and his excitement. Even his hair and beard seemed to catch the white glitter of the snow. He was a resplendent figure on his fine horse, Crosswhite thought, with his fur-collared greatcoat and his polished Wellington boots and the soft felt hat curling in the wind. A fine figure. Why should

Crosswhite be examining so many doubts about him now, facing questions he had shunted aside before?

"They won't bother us," he said. "They like easy pickings."

He led the single file of white hunters across the snow, watching for any signs of agitation that would tell him the buffaloes had detected them. The heavier, slower-moving bulls were at the rear of the drove, the fleeter cows leading the way. He would have to try to turn one of those cows.

They were still two hundred yards away when a few of the cows and younger bulls on the fringes of the herd began to gallop back and forth, their excitement showing that they had sensed danger. The herd was slow in its response—they were such easy targets, Crosswhite thought, as he urged his sorrel into a run. Maybe Bill Cody didn't have so much to brag about.

Then there was little time for thought.

The small herd broke into two smaller parts as the riders charged close. Crosswhite rode right through the twin packs and broke to the front. Drifting left, he managed to swing outside one of the lead cows. Then he moved in, crowding her, forcing her into a broad swing to the right.

The panicking herd followed her, quickly forming a long, curving formation like the sweep of a scythe. The muffled drumming of hoofs and the clattering of buffalo horns drowned out all other sound. The air was dense with clouds of the light, powdery snow, thick as dust, half-obscuring the charging buffaloes and the pursuing riders.

Crosswhite heard the crash of a rifle, then another, but he did not look behind. He swung left, reined in hard, and skidded from the sorrel's back in almost the same motion. Dropping to his knees, he picked out a mature bull at the edge of the drove and tumbled him with a single shot that struck just where the shaggy mane ended and penetrated the heart.

The excitement and turmoil whirled away from him. Crosswhite ignored it. He rode closer to the fallen bull and made sure he was dead. Alighting once more, he tied his horse's reins lightly to the buffalo's horns before he set about the business of methodically cutting up the animal. He took no pride in what he had done, nor did he feel any reluctance over butchering the dead animal. It was nothing to think about.

He was busy, and if he felt an oblique surprise over the continuing sounds of gunfire, he thought little of that either. Most of the shooting was from terrain no longer visible to him, the buffaloes and the hunters having disappeared over a swelling of the plain. The herd had been caught in a flat bottom where they often liked to graze. Maybe Leland Hubbard wasn't as accurate as he thought with that old buffalo rifle, if he had to take so many shots.

When Crosswhite had finished cutting away the best meat and packing it in the skin, he rose and moved away, exercising muscles in his legs that had begun to stiffen while he squatted. He washed his knife and his gloves in the snow.

There was silence all around him now. The shooting was over. How long had it been since they first charged into the herd? Less than an hour, surely. Not much more than half that.

He left the fresh meat on the ground by the remains of the carcass, although he knew that he couldn't leave it for long with that pack of wolves so close by. One of Hubbard's wagons was following the hunters to pick up the fresh meat. It should be nearby.

Crosswhite rode to the top of the rise over which the fleeing herd had disappeared. He was unprepared for the sight that greeted him, and the shock of it made him pull up sharply.

The land fell away in a broad, slanting table toward the southeast. Scattered across that purity of white for a distance of a mile or more was what seemed like the entire buffalo herd. No more than half a dozen could have escaped. The dead made small patches of black and red half-sunken in the snow.

In the distance riders rode back and forth in what seemed like a frenzied dance of excitement, occasionally scored by rifle fire. But there was no longer anything to shoot at. Across all that white plain there was nothing moving or alive except the tiny figures of the hunters on their horses.

Crosswhite did not move. In time several of the distant riders galloped back toward him.

Leland Hubbard, followed by a grinning Rossiter and Vorec, standing grimly in his stirrups, loped up to Crosswhite and reined in. Hubbard's horse threw up a cascade of snow and skidded dangerously from the reckless speed of his run across that deceptively soft terrain. Crosswhite had the odd expectation of seeing the entrepreneur spattered with the blood of his kill, but he was unmarked. His red face was flushed to a more vivid color with exuberance.

"Your West can be tamed, Mr. Crosswhite," he roared triumphantly. "It can be brought down to its knees, and I've done it this day!"

"I thought you were after meat," Crosswhite said coldly. "Or a chance to say you brought down a buffalo with your Cody rifle. But this—" He had no words for the senseless slaughter spread before them.

"A dozen of them!" Leland Hubbard exulted as if he had not heard. "I brought down a dozen at least by my own hand. If there'd been more, I'd have given Mr. Cody a run for his money. By Jove, that was splendid! And much credit to you and that horse of yours, Mr. Crosswhite. He did his work handsomely. If you'd care to sell him, sir, you can name your price."

"He's not for sale."

"The other, then? That dun? Is she as good at her work?"

"No," Crosswhite answered curtly, though the temptation to see Hubbard try to ride the claybank at that moment was strong. He had brought her along only as a pack horse, and to save a livery stable bill in his absence from Cheyenne.

The cold manner of his replies did not penetrate Leland Hubbard's excitement. "I didn't see you after the first charge, Mr. Crosswhite. Where were you?"

"I shot a bull. He's cut up and waiting."

The two cavalrymen, Austin and Jamison, had reached them by then. In the distance the hunter called Roget had begun to butcher some of the fallen buffalo. As Crosswhite stared, a wagon lumbered over the crest to his right and started down the long incline toward the scattered remains of the herd.

"Cut up? Yes, of course, we can use some fresh meat. There'll be choice cuts to go around, eh?" The joy of the chase still glittered in Hubbard's eyes. "But it's the heads I want. Only the finest, of course. I'll have something extra to show for this expedition. A capital hunt, Mr. Crosswhite! You can be sure I won't forget it!"

Crosswhite wondered how many times Hubbard had assured him that neither he nor the world would forget this expedition. As Hubbard rode to intercept the wagon, the others following, Crosswhite looked after them in disgust. What was he doing in this company? He could almost hear Annie Macauley asking the question, and he had no answer that did not make his disgust turn inward.

Turning back toward his own kill, he heard the wolves. They scattered when they saw him. Already they had stolen most of the meat he had packed.

Well, let them have it, Crosswhite thought. They would have a feast this day to make their bellies drag in the snow.

The wolves watched him from a rim as he rode away. Some of them barked in hungry frustration. One threw back his head and howled.

Before he was out of sight they began to slink toward the torn carcass, circling closer like a noose tightening. The snarls followed Crosswhite as the wolves began to fight among themselves.

23

"I gather you didn't approve, Mr. Crosswhite."

Crosswhite glanced up at Captain Arthur Austin, but he made no reply.

They had camped on the banks of the narrow little creek called the Chugwater, which flowed north into the Laramie River and east from there into the North Fork of the Platte. It was dark, and the camp was quiet. Hubbard was in his tent, still rehashing the day's success. One of the wagons had been largely cleared to make room for six of the finest buffalo heads Hubbard meant to take back East as trophies.

"You're a Westerner," Austin said. "You've killed game before."

"Yep."

"And you must have killed for sport."

"Sometimes."

After a moment Austin said, "You think this hunt today was different."

Crosswhite grunted. He was not sure exactly why the pointless wasting of the herd had left him disgruntled not only with Leland Hubbard but with himself. Was it only the way Hubbard had begun to bother him? Hell's fire, he had seen far more buffaloes cut down by hunters for their skins.

Hubbard had left the skins and most of the meat to rot, or to feed the wolves. It was only those half-dozen heads he'd been interested in.

He killed to talk about it.

"It's different for you, of course," Austin mused. "None of it is new to you, I suppose. I'll confess to being excited myself during the chase. What great shaggy creatures they are when they're on the run! I won't forget that."

"You takin' back a head?"

Austin flushed, either at the suggestion or at Crosswhite's tone. "No." He studied Crosswhite in the darkness. They were some distance from the fire, and it was impossible to read Crosswhite's face. "I suppose we killed more than we needed to. . . ."

"That's one reason you're still fighting Indians," Crosswhite said pointedly. "Those animals mean somethin' to the Indians. They mean nothin' at all to a man like Hubbard."

"Yes, I see." Strange sentiments for a Westerner, the captain thought, although he saw that Crosswhite's remark made a kind of sense. "Have you dealt much with Indians? You know them well?"

"Not so well."

"I was wondering about your encounter with White Wolf. I mean, the way you stayed with him until he died, and gave him . . . last respects, so to speak."

He waited so long that he thought Crosswhite was not going to answer. Then he said, "I reckon that says it about as well as it can be said. Last respects."

"Yes, but—"

"He was a man, Captain. Maybe a hell of a good one, from what I hear."

"A savage—"

"What does that mean? That he didn't have Christianity, like you and me and Mr. Hubbard? You talk about respectin' things. That Indian had respect for everythin' he touched and used, for the animals he killed and the ones he rode— but did you see the way Hubbard's horse was latherin' after that chase? An Indian respects the wind and the snow and the land, same as he respects any man who fights him hard in battle, the way he fights." Crosswhite broke off, surprised by the heat of his own outburst, by words he had not known were in his mind. "Yep, I paid him last respects. I doubt he would've done the same for me, but that's only because he didn't think the same way. If he thought I was a brave warrior like him, he'd have shown respect in his own way, not ours." Crosswhite smiled thinly. "Like leavin' me my hair, or not cuttin' off any parts."

Captain Arthur Austin nodded slowly, acknowledging the justice of what he had heard, yet puzzled still. Finally he voiced the question uppermost in his mind. "I wonder why you're here, Mr. Crosswhite."

Crosswhite looked at him sharply. "You know why."

"Yes, I suppose . . . the reward."

"Anythin' wrong with that?" Crosswhite demanded.

"No, not at all. It's just—"

"Every man draws his wages for what he does. Like you, Captain." Crosswhite realized that he was being belligerent, reacting angrily to the soldier's mild comment, which had held more curiosity than rebuke.

There was irony in Austin's smile. "Ordinarily that might be so, Mr. Crosswhite. Unfortunately, in this circumstance it isn't."

"What's that mean?"

"It seems there are some congressmen—a majority, that is—who believe the Army is too large and too expensive. In addition to stopping all promotions above my rank, the Congress has neglected, by oversight or determination, to appropriate any funds for Army pay this year."

Crosswhite could only gape at him.

"Enlisted men draw food and clothing," Austin went on.

"But in this year of Our Lord eighteen hundred and seventy-eight, the officers of the United States Army are self-supporting." The heavy irony dropped from his tone. "It isn't so bad for someone like myself—I have some limited funds. But a married man like Lieutenant Schaefer has been hard put to get along on borrowed money. Borrowed at interest, Mr. Crosswhite."

Crosswhite shook his head. All the belligerence he had briefly felt was gone. Austin's revelation that he served without pay—that, in fact, he had drawn no pay for the skirmish in which White Wolf was wounded—somehow seemed to throw Crosswhite's eager money-grubbing for the reward Hubbard offered into an even harsher light.

He looked up to find Captain Austin staring thoughtfully toward the wagon that now carried the six shaggy trophies of the day's hunt. "Do you know Mr. Hubbard's plans?" Austin asked.

"No." He hadn't pressed the Easterner, Crosswhite thought. Maybe he hadn't wanted to know too much. All he had wanted to be sure about was that reward.

"I suggest you ask him, Mr. Crosswhite," Austin said. "He told me you were going East with him."

"There was some such talk, but nothin' was settled."

Austin rose. "We should find White Wolf before sunset tomorrow, if your guess is right. I think you ought to know what Hubbard means to do with him before then."

Crosswhite watched the likable young officer

walk toward his own tent, his shadow wavering among the deeper shadows of the trees that sheltered the creekside flank of the camp.

I didn't want to know, he thought. And I don't now. But Austin was right. He had to find out. He had to find out because there was an ugly feeling in his gut that told him he already knew.

Austin had almost reached his tent when a brash young recruit from Philadelphia—he was no more than a boy, and the horse he had mounted for the first time after enlisting in the cavalry was the first horse he had ever ridden in his life—charged out of the snow and the darkness and stumbled toward him. "Sir! Captain Austin, sir—"

"Easy, easy—Private Regan, isn't it?"

"Yes, sir. Oh, my God—!"

"What is it, Regan? Take a deep breath and tell it slow."

Regan gulped in a breath as if on command. "It's Private Dawkins, sir. The forward sentry—he's dead, sir. Sergeant Jamison says it's Indians!"

Austin was on the run before the private had finished talking, aiming for the pickets that had been set for the horses along the banks of the creek. He was aware of a rising commotion around him, of men running through the ill-lit darkness in different directions, as if without purpose. There had been cavalry sentries at each end of the picket line, and a civilian—one of Hubbard's scouts, posted by previous agreement for the expedition—guarding the southerly point of the camp.

From somewhere nearby came an excited shout: "Indians!"

Austin swore. He could have a panic on his hands. He hadn't anticipated an attack—there had been no sign of hostiles anywhere along the trail. If not sleeping, the sentry must have been careless.

Should he order the men out? No, Jamison would have sounded the alarm instead of sending a messenger if the camp were threatened.

The sentry had been found at his post beyond the picket line. Sergeant Jamison was on the scene when Austin pounded up, breathing hard and painfully. Jamison rose without hurry. Suddenly Austin was glad of Jamison's experience, the seasoned calm that never left him, even in battle. If the sergeant ever raised his voice to flay the hide of an unlucky recruit, it was a deliberate uproar.

"It's Private Dawkins, sir," he said.

"Scalped?"

"No, sir."

"What happened?"

"There are some tracks, Captain. Moccasins show up good in this snow, so we know it was hostiles. I'd guess they might've been after the horses. There was two of 'em, judgin' by the tracks. Regan heard Dawkins call out once, and that made 'em run. We can thank Dawkins for that."

The sentry had been stabbed in the back, and when he made an outcry, the knife blade had slashed his throat and cut off the warning. There had been a lot of bleeding. In the darkness a few feet away someone was vomiting into the snow. Somehow that seemed worse than being sick on bare ground. The dead sentry was lightly clad, and it was a moment before Captain Austin realized that his winter fur had probably been stolen. Jamison confirmed the theft of the coat, along with Dawkins' forage cap and rifle.

Austin glanced up from the trooper's body at the commotion that signaled the arrival of Leland Hubbard. Crosswhite and others were among the men crowding close.

"Double the guard, sergeant," Austin said.

"Yes, sir."

"You're here to give us protection," Leland Hubbard said unnecessarily, raising his voice.

"You'll have it," Austin snapped, stifling his resentment. It was not one of Hubbard's people who had died.

Lee Crosswhite looked from the officer to Hubbard. He said, "Looks like you ain't got your West tamed after all, Mr. Hubbard."

The impresario started to bluster, but apparently

changed his mind. He had eaten well, and now he looked unhappy, his florid face seeming paler, like the dead sentry's. "Why did they do it?" he managed to say.

"I'd guess the sergeant's right. They was after the horses."

"Why would they let us know they're out there?" Hubbard stared uneasily into the impenetrable darkness beyond the trees. "I mean, if they plan to attack us . . ."

"We don't know that they plan any such thing," Captain Austin said crisply. "Chances are against it. We don't know of any Indian force at large that is strong enough to attack us." Unless Little Wolf had come down from Montana, he thought. "All we know is that two Indians tried to steal some horses. In any event, rumors and idle speculation won't help. If you'll have your men withdraw, Mr. Hubbard, I think we can all use a good night's sleep. We'll know a lot better what's ahead for us in the morning."

Slowly the gaping circle pulled back, breaking up, but it was a long time—long after the dead sentry's body had been wrapped in blankets and carried to one of the wagons—before the little knots of talkers loosened and the camp at last was quiet.

In his own blankets Lee Crosswhite lay awake, staring upward through naked branches at a sky that was low and black, unrelieved by any stars.

183

The wind blowing down the valley was gusty and cold. Storm's coming, he thought. But it was not the threat of weather, nor the sudden danger from hostiles, that kept him awake. He was facing the motives that had brought him to this camp beside the creek, less than a day's ride from that older camp where White Wolf had come to die, and he didn't much like what he saw.

He'd had a few setbacks, that was all. They had piled up on him until he got to feeling sorry for himself. That was what Annie Macauley had seen, and it explained her anger. He had asked her to marry him not because he'd known that was what he wanted but because he'd been brooding so long over his misfortunes that he was ready to grasp at any refuge. Hell's fire, Annie was what he wanted, right enough, but he hadn't known how much until she said no.

Things were never as bad as a man tired or scared was tempted to paint them. He could always scrape an existence from the land, even in winter. He could feed himself, keep himself warm, survive, until there came another spring.

He wished Annie had been there so he could tell her, but he had gotten himself into another kind of company.

And he was liking that less and less.

24

Sergeant Jamison and Roget, the civilian scout, were sent out at first light to run down the trail of the two Indian raiders. They followed the tracks until they disappeared along the rocky bed of the creek. Searching up- and downstream, after a half hour they found the natural shelter where two unshod ponies had been tethered. The pony tracks cut a double trail across the snow until they vanished on a rocky table swept clear by strong winds. The continuing gusts made dubious the value of a long pursuit, and the scouts returned to the camp.

A meeting was held in Hubbard's tent over breakfast. The group included Austin and Lieutenant Schaefer, Jamison, Crosswhite, Hubbard, Rossiter, and the ever-present dwarf, Vorec.

"You're determined to go on, Mr. Hubbard?" Austin asked after the scouts' report was heard.

"Certainly, sir. You've already given me your opinion that the hostiles are no threat."

"I didn't say that exactly. I said I didn't know of a force in this region large enough to attack an expedition of our size."

"It's the same thing, Captain."

Austin shrugged. He was not a contentious

man, Lee Crosswhite thought, but he was level-headed and clear-thinking.

"Then you must consider this, Mr. Hubbard. If you mean to leave the wagons here and return to them, I'll have to divide my detachment, leaving some of my men—and some of yours as well—as a guard. Once our forces are split, we'll be more vulnerable to attack—or at any rate a band of renegades might think so."

"Are you suggesting that you *cannot* offer adequate protection to this expedition, Captain? I should think your superiors must have considered the possible necessity of guarding a base camp as well as a search party in the field."

"I'm not suggesting that at all," Austin said stiffly. "Only that the risk is increased, and that is a consideration you must face." The killing of the sentry continued to puzzle him. Even though he was not ready to believe in a large war party plotting an attack, he was uneasy about dividing his escort. Hubbard was foolish to be scornful of the Indian threat. He had not fought them.

"We're going on as planned," Hubbard declared. "A few cowardly savages sneaking into our camp under cover of darkness aren't going to frighten us off when we're so close to the prize."

"Might be more than a few cowards," Crosswhite suggested quietly. The others all looked at him in surprise, Rossiter with fresh dislike. "We're here lookin' for White Wolf's body. It could be some of his relatives are huntin' for the same thing." His eyes met Hubbard's. "They might have found him 'fore this. He was a great chief, and his kin and followers wouldn't much like the notion of his body fallin' into our hands. Leastwise, most Indians feel that way, and he was as big a war-leader as they had still fightin'."

"That makes sense, Captain," young Schaefer put in eagerly. "It would explain a bunch of renegades venturing this far south toward Cheyenne City. It would explain stealing horses, too. After all, we found White Wolf's horse. An eye for an eye—it would be like them."

"That's possible," Captain Austin admitted, but he did not sound convinced. A leaderless band of warriors plotting vengeance seemed farfetched.

"I was wonderin' when you'd try to weasel out," Sut Rossiter drawled, his mocking gaze on Crosswhite.

Hubbard turned toward him. "What do you mean, Mr. Rossiter?"

"You know damned well what I mean and so does he. I told you all along he never seen that Indian, dead or alive. He was only tryin' to get hisself that reward. Now we're within spittin' distance of that place where he says he buried the savage, and all of a sudden he starts to thinkin' about some relatives sneakin' off with the body." Rossiter's big teeth flashed. "He can't take us to no body if it's been stole."

187

Crosswhite felt the lash of anger. "You said that for the last time."

"You want some more ribs busted, drifter? Or just quick lead? I been savin' it—"

"Stop this!" Leland Hubbard roared. It was the bellow of a ringmaster, and inside the tent it was effective enough to silence the two angry enemies. "I've had your word, Mr. Rossiter. You'll put up your quarrel, or you'll leave this company at once!"

Rossiter flushed, but he checked his quick retort. He didn't like taking orders from Hubbard, Crosswhite thought, but he must have his own reward to come.

Hubbard had bought a lot with his promised gold.

"It's settled then, gentlemen," Leland Hubbard announced when he was sure that his warning had been taken. "We're going on. Show us the way, Mr. Crosswhite!"

Throughout that morning's ride Lee Crosswhite thought about Leland Hubbard's ready promises. He also found himself remembering what Captain Austin had said: *We should find White Wolf tomorrow. You ought to know what Hubbard means to do with him before then.*

What *did* Hubbard mean to do? How could finding one dead Indian chief's body be worth so much to him—enough to promise a huge reward, and to hold out tantalizing vistas of unexplained fame and wealth?

Whatever it was, he wanted no part of it. But how to back out of his commitment now? The thought of confirming Sut Rossiter's accusation for any reason cut deeply—too deeply. In a couple of hours more he could prove that he hadn't lied.

The search party had been climbing the sloping breast of the foothills, but what lay ahead was not softness but the hard, massive black bulk of the mountains themselves, broken not by gentle dips and valleys but huge, raw cuts and canyons like deep wounds.

One section of bluffs was different, its high peaks ragged, its long flanks distinctively pink in coloration. There were canyons here, too. Near the mouth of one of them Crosswhite had laid White Wolf in the arms of a pine tree. And he had described the pink bluffs earlier to both Hubbard and Austin.

The discovery of this landmark, though still more than an hour's ride away, put Leland Hubbard into high humor. A short time later he stopped the expedition for lunch, in spite of the fact that they were in the open, exposed to the cutting edge of the wind, which had been in their faces all morning. From the saddlebags of a pack mule Hubbard produced several bottles of sparkling champagne and held them triumphantly aloft.

"A superb wine to celebrate our success, gentlemen," he announced. "Chilled to perfection by the elements. As you see, Captain Austin, your worries were groundless. Here's a drink to tame your savage plains, Mr. Crosswhite, and even a soothing beverage to compose a quarrel, eh?"

Not everyone drank. It was like officers only, Crosswhite saw, with the enlisted troopers and most of Hubbard's entourage left out, excepting Rossiter and himself. Vorec, the entrepreneur's little aide, poured champagne into goblets and passed them around to each privileged man. It was a strange way to celebrate anything on these high plains in the middle of winter, with the wind kicking up the snow all around them and gray clouds scudding swiftly overhead. It was certainly the first bunch he had ever joined in which the leader insisted on pausing for a lunch of smoked fish and cheeses and sparkling wine.

Crosswhite waited until the odd repast had been eaten and he saw Hubbard striding alone toward his horse to get one of his cigars. Vorec could not reach high enough to fetch them easily. Crosswhite hurried after the white-haired leader of the expedition.

"Ah, Mr. Crosswhite! You'll have a cigar?"

"No, Mr. Hubbard. There's somethin' I been meanin' to ask, that's all."

"Ask away. I'll find it hard to deny you anything you ask of me this day, Mr. Crosswhite."

"I suppose I should have figgered it out from what you told me, about how folks back East is curious over redskins. But I'd like to hear you kinda spell it out."

"Why certainly, sir." Hubbard smiled. "My guess is you want to know what part you have in my plans. I told you, Mr. Crosswhite, I'd make you famous if you took me to White Wolf, and I mean to keep my word. It's a 'Wild West' show I'm going to take on tour, but this will be different from anything ever seen before. We'll visit the great cities of this country and even beyond its shores. We'll take our show to London, England, Mr. Crosswhite. You'll ride before the Queen of England herself! I'll make you a hero as celebrated as Buffalo Bill Cody himself—and you know in what esteem I hold that great gentleman!"

Hubbard was going to do it all, Crosswhite thought. There was nothing said about what Crosswhite might do, other than what he was told. He had a sudden unpleasing picture of himself being talked about by Hubbard as "my man," like Vorec. He had the dwarf along as an exhibit, perhaps one that enhanced his own stature. Crosswhite would be another showpiece, a real live western character on horseback, a bit high-smelling maybe, but not dangerous if you knew how to handle him.

"It wasn't myself I was wonderin' about, Mr. Hubbard. It was White Wolf."

Leland Resurrection Hubbard beamed at him. "I want his head, Mr. Crosswhite! Don't you understand? It will be the prize trophy to exhibit in our show. Mark my words, sir, there will be a hundred thousand people—no, more than that—five, ten times as many as that will pay handsomely to see that savage king's head. In this country alone! And as many more across the seas. Others have tried it, sir, but never with a warrior so famed, so dreaded as White Wolf of the Sioux Nation. And never with the manner of promotion I mean to provide. Mr. Crosswhite, before I'm done there won't be a man or woman in the civilized world who won't have heard White Wolf's name, and wished to be among those fortunate enough to glimpse that noble head!"

Crosswhite shuddered in a spasm of self-disgust. Next to the grudging respect for a dying man's courage and dignity, the impulse that had kept him at White Wolf's side in his last hours and caused him to give the Indian a kind of burial ceremony, next to that the greed that had brought him to this moment at Leland Hubbard's side shriveled him.

That was what Annie meant, he thought. That's why she was surprised.

He had come within a hair of betraying not only White Wolf's humanity, but his own.

"I'll have no part of it," he said slowly.

"Eh? What's that, Mr. Crosswhite? I don't understand."

Crosswhite had shot at more than one Indian, and he might very well hold another in his sights again. But right now he knew that he was closer to a man like White Wolf than he was to Hubbard and Rossiter and their kind, with their contempt for all things living, for animals and people, red or white.

"I didn't know it was a trophy you wanted," he said, "like one of your buffalo heads to mount on the wall. It was my mistake, Mr. Hubbard."

"What are you saying, sir?" Hubbard's habitual smiling expression had changed, but there was no real concern in his eyes, simply a different kind of amusement. "Surely you aren't concerned over the likes of that savage. Why, he'd as soon rip the hair off your own head as look at you!"

"That may be—"

"What's different, Mr. Crosswhite? For me to mount my trophy, as you put it, though with dubious accuracy, or for that heathen to fly your hair from his lance or hang it on a string for all his people to see? It's all the same, sir, all the same."

Was it? Were these childish qualms he was feeling, without substance? Slowly he shook his head. When an Indian stole the hair of a brave enemy, he took that fighting man's spirit to bolster his own. When he flew hair on his lance it was an act of pride, not greed. He said, "It's not the same, Mr. Hubbard."

"Have you forgotten what manner of man we're speaking of?" Hubbard flared in sudden anger. "Have you so soon forgotten the atrocities that savage has committed on your own kind? He was at Little Big Horn, Mr. Crosswhite! Have you forgotten those brave soldiers?"

"He won't be killing any more soldiers," Crosswhite answered evenly. "He's dead."

"And all his sins forgiven him?"

"I don't know. I'm not in the forgiving business. And I'm not in the trophy business, neither, nor the circus business."

Leland Hubbard stared at him, all humor gone. "You'd better make yourself clear, Mr. Crosswhite."

"I thought I done that. I'll tell it plain. I've brought you as far as I mean to."

Hubbard's mouth dropped open. "You can't mean what you're saying."

"You talk fine, Mr. Hubbard, but you don't listen very good."

"Have *you* listened to anything I've said? The future that can be yours—are you blind to all that?"

"It ain't me."

"Then what *is* you, Mr. Crosswhite?" Hubbard

194

demanded angrily. "The food in your belly? I provided it. The saddle on your horse? It wouldn't be yours today but for the gold I put in your palm. The tobacco you smoke, the drinks you've enjoyed—all mine, Mr. Crosswhite. My gifts to you! You owe me for that."

Crosswhite nodded reluctantly. "I reckon there's truth in that. You'll be paid for every crumb of tobacco. Even for that champagne."

"I'll not have it, Mr. Crosswhite," the entrepreneur roared. "You can't lead me this far and then crawl out on your word. Mr. Rossiter!"

Crosswhite felt a sharp chill. Suddenly he understood more clearly another thing that had puzzled him—Sut Rossiter's role in Leland Hubbard's expedition. Hubbard planned for every contingency, including any that might require the backing of a fast gun.

"Mr. Rossiter!" the impresario shouted again, his face red, as the gunman ran toward them. "Mr. Crosswhite says he'll have no further part in our expedition."

Rossiter's big teeth flashed. "That's what I've been waiting to hear."

"Not yet, Mr. Rossiter. I simply want you to persuade Mr. Crosswhite that he'll be better advised to keep his word. I've come this far, sir," Hubbard said, addressing Crosswhite now. "Nothing is going to stop me—no man's duplicity or weakness."

"You'd best not say that again, Mr. Hubbard," Crosswhite said softly. "One time I'll take it you mean somebody else."

"I mean you, Mr. Crosswhite, and no mistake!" Hubbard's face was the red of blood on snow, like the blood of those slaughtered buffaloes. The florid skin had been burned by sun and wind and snow glare even before anger came to heighten the color. "You are either a potential thief or a blackguard, sir, but I'll not let you turn tail on me now. Mr. Rossiter, see to it! I want him alive— and at the point of this expedition until we sight White Wolf's grave!"

A possibility nudged the edge of Crosswhite's mind, eluding him when he tried to seize and examine it. Leland Hubbard was acting out of character. Something was wrong, something Crosswhite had felt in his gut before this moment, a premonition of danger so vague as to be easily dismissed.

"We don't need you no longer, Crosswhite," Rossiter said with a grin. He looked as if he didn't much care whether Crosswhite stayed alive as Hubbard urged or not. "Roget says he knows those hills and he can find that creek where you camped without you to point it out, now we can see the bluffs. I reckon you know what that means."

Crosswhite's gaze flicked toward Leland Hubbard. The red-faced impresario stared back at him, his eyes cold. They've talked of this before, Crosswhite suddenly knew.

"You're mine now," Rossiter said. "You been hidin' behind that dead Injun as long as you can."

Then it was all clear. There was more collusion between Hubbard and Rossiter than he had guessed. Hubbard might be free with his champagne, but he was also a greedy man— not the kind to hand out five hundred dollars in gold to a man who would soon be dead anyway, unable to spend it. Once he was apprised of the enmity between Crosswhite and Rossiter, he would have made that fact a part of his plans. He'd never intended to pay that reward. That was why he had made sure everyone in the expedition knew of the quarrel between the two men. No other explanation would be needed for Crosswhite's death when it came. Not even Captain Austin would be able to bring charges against Rossiter for the settlement of a private quarrel long postponed. Perhaps Rossiter had even been promised a share of the gold for doing what he intended to do all along: kill Crosswhite as soon as his knowledge was no longer essential.

And that moment had come.

By this time the erupting clash had drawn the attention of the entire search party. From the corner of his eye Crosswhite saw Captain Austin hurrying toward them. He did not risk a glance that way. One crack would be all the opening Sut Rossiter needed.

"Back on your horse, Crosswhite," Rossiter ordered. "If you want to breathe a little longer."

Crosswhite shook his head. "A man who'd cheat at cards like you done would shoot me in the back as quick. I'll not turn my back to you."

The mocking laughter left Rossiter's cold eyes. "Then you'll have it in the belly."

The heavy click of a rifle hammer broke between them, followed by another and another. "Drop your guns, Mr. Rossiter," Austin commanded sharply. "You too, Mr. Crosswhite."

Startled, neither man moved to obey. But now Crosswhite saw that Austin was flanked by Sergeant Jamison and three other troopers. All had their rifles cocked and ready to fire on command. Two of them were youngsters, Crosswhite noted, but the set of their jaws—even the hint of fear in their eyes—said clearly that they would shoot at their captain's word.

"Withdraw your men," Leland Hubbard bristled. "This is not your affair, Captain Austin."

"There'll be no shooting while this expedition is under my protection," Austin answered, unruffled. "What any of you do afterward is not my concern, but for now—I wouldn't advise it, Mr. Rossiter! You'll have the Army to answer to if any one of my troopers is shot."

"You'll hear about this, Captain!" Leland

Hubbard raged. "I have friends in Washington—"

"In Congress?" Austin snapped back. "I don't feel too friendly toward the Congress right now, Mr. Hubbard. Your threats are empty. Are you going to drop those guns, Mr. Rossiter, or must I have my men take them from you?"

"I have other guns I can call!" Hubbard roared in baffled outrage.

"And I have two for every one of them," Austin said calmly. "If you believe I won't use them as necessary, Mr. Hubbard, you will not have judged me well."

How long the stalemate would have lasted, or who would have acted to break it, Crosswhite would never know. While the angry triangle held taut—Crosswhite alone at one point, Rossiter at another, Captain Austin and his men confronting both of them—one of the troopers sang out.

"Captain Austin, sir—rider from the wagons!"

25

Lieutenant Ernest Schaefer had been forced to conceal his disappointment over being left behind with the wagons. He was convinced that any attack by the Indians, if one was to come at all, would strike at the troopers in the field, not at the wagons. If it came he would be left out of it.

Schaefer was twenty-five years old—too young to have fought in the War between the States. The skirmish with White Wolf's hunting party had been the first real military action of his brief career. Now, weeks later, the memory of that night before the battle, the stomach-churning excitement of anticipation and fear, and the heart-hammering moment in the morning when the savages on their ponies burst clear of the trees and into the clear line of fire of Schaefer and his men on the bluff, all that was as vivid to him as if it had taken place yesterday. He thought of it now as the high point of his life. That was what he had been waiting and working for, even dreaming about since he was a ten-year-old and his older brother Tom was fighting with the Pennsylvanians. He had even envied Tom his limp when he came home after the war. He had never understood his brother's apparent indifference to questions about the war, his reluctance to talk about the fighting, about what battles he had fought in and how many Rebs he had shot. Tom had acted as if all he wanted to do was forget it all.

Well, Ernest Schaefer would have something to talk about when he went home on leave. Even back in Pennsylvania they had heard of White Wolf of the Sioux.

Schaefer had posted sentries—two of his ten troopers and one of Hubbard's men, all six of whom were grizzled Westerners ten and fifteen years older than Schaefer, who accepted his orders with tolerant amusement; but he doubted their necessity. The four wagons were boxed to create a defensive position almost like a fort. The horses not taken with the search party had been drawn within the square as a precaution that gave credit to the Indians' midnight raid. The trees along the creek, which ran south to north, offered cover in that direction, but the area to the south and east was open, sloping away from the camp to lower levels. Nothing moved across that white expanse. Nothing could move without being seen. There would be no threat from that open plain without ample warning. Two points of Schaefer's watch had therefore been assigned to the northern perimeter of the camp, one to the south.

His knowledge of Indian tactics was sketchy. It was soon to be increased.

The creek wound its narrow way along a shallow trough south of the camp, a wriggling depression that was easily visible for a quarter-mile or more across the snow-covered plain. The absence of cover—there was not even much brush along the banks of the stream—caused Schaefer to dismiss it as a possible source of danger. But even if he had been looking for them there, he would not have seen the Indians until they were almost upon the camp. They wore whitened deerskins pulled over their heads and shoulders as they crawled along the creek bed. The white blended into the white vastness of the snowfield—an expanse so great that, even under gray and threatening skies, it hurt the eyes, further compounding the difficulty of seeing anything clearly in that terrain.

All this Draws-Out-Arrows had foreseen and counted on when he planned the attack.

There was no warning until the first shot.

It seemed to come from nowhere. Lieutenant Schaefer turned toward the white emptiness south of the camp in astonishment, distrusting his senses. He heard a sentry's shout of warning. Then there was a small volley of fire, the sounds remarkably thin as if the snow had muffled them.

And Schaefer saw puffs of smoke along the rim of the creek.

He swung toward the wagons. As he shouted his first orders he saw a young trooper drop his rifle and clutch his throat with both hands. At the same moment snowy apparitions rose from the shallow defile to the south like white-sheeted ghosts. Another volley of rifle fire crackled thinly.

By this time the troopers were returning a ragged fire. Schaefer ordered them toward the protection of the four boxed wagons. The attention of the two forward sentries, along with that of the entire camp, had been diverted to the rear by the noise of the attack.

Lieutenant Schaefer had almost reached the wagons when the main thrust of the Indian attack came, led by Wounded Heel. It came from the north.

This time the hostiles struck in more predictable fashion—at least more like Lieutenant Schaefer's imagined picture of an Indian assault. They swooped from the trees on horseback, shrilling war cries that chilled the blood of recruits who had never heard those screams before. It was a furious charge, so swift and unexpected that some of the gaping troopers forgot to trigger their weapons. Schaefer could not have said how many were in that first wave that spilled over the bank of the creek and burst through the trees to engulf the camp. There was too much noise and confusion. As he vaulted behind the cover of a wagon wheel and dropped flat to the ground, it seemed to him that a wave of painted savages would wash right over the soldiers' position. Then the wave broke around the square of wagons to the left and right. Each flank curled quickly back and away, retreating to the cover of the trees and the higher bank of the creek.

Not a single Indian had been hit by the erratic fire of the white defenders. One of Hubbard's men had been nicked in the arm. One trooper, Private Foster, was badly wounded, probably dying from a bullet in the lung.

A kind of numbness began to recede from Lieutenant Ernest Schaefer's brain. He was vaguely surprised to note that he had felt no fear. The attack had been too sudden, too surprising.

Belatedly he realized that he had been careless. He had been foolishly convinced that the Indians would be interested only in the main body of the expedition. Moreover, he had underestimated the enemy—an unforgivable mistake. He had given them little credit for imaginative, unpredictable tactics.

"I want three men behind each wagon," he heard himself ordering crisply. "We don't know where they'll come from next time, so I want four men—you, Dodson, Kennedy, McDonald, and you, Mr. Wills"—the last-named was one of Hubbard's entourage—"to be at the ready with me. We'll shift to meet the attack, whichever direction it comes from."

This was not the same as that first taste of battle,

he thought as he waited. He could feel the blood beating in his eyes and ears, almost painful, but there was not the heady excitement he had felt on the bluff during that last hour before dawn. In its place was a cold, solid lump in his stomach that seemed to want to force its way up into his throat. You had it all your own way the last time, he told himself. It wasn't any real fight at all. This time those hostiles are looking down the barrel at you.

He was scared, but he also felt a new pride over the way he had kept his head and coolly given orders to prepare for the coming assault.

Maybe he would yet make a real soldier after all.

He wondered suddenly if he would be so anxious to talk about it, presuming he lived to do so, or would he end up like Tom, silent and haunted?

In the space of a half-hour there were two more sudden, whirlwind attacks from the cover to the north. Each time the Indians circled the box of wagons and returned to the trees, firing as they went, many of them hanging on the far side of their ponies so you could find no target to shoot at. Remarkably no one on either side seemed to have been hit in these exchanges. At least there were no fresh casualties among the defenders behind their effective barricades, and there were no Indian bodies sprawled out there on the snow.

Schaefer was unable to get any clear count of

the number of savages besieging the wagons. The estimates of the force in the first attack varied from a dozen mounted hostiles to as many as three times that, depending on the witness. There was no certain tally of the snipers in the creekbed to the south, who had remained in their position. Schaefer's own estimate was about five or six men under those white skins in the creekbed, and another dozen in each of the mounted attacks. But it now seemed unlikely that the Indian leader had committed all of his forces yet. Lieutenant Ernest Schaefer was not about to underestimate his enemy a second time.

He needed help. If the hostiles decided to launch an attack in full force, the wagons might be overrun.

"Corporal Houghton!" he called.

A skinny, goose-necked soldier came on the run, his head bobbing on the long neck. "Sir!"

"That bay of yours, will he run well in the snow?"

Corporal Houghton grinned. "He'll fly like a snow goose, Lieutenant."

Schaefer considered. The bay gelding was the fastest horse there—Houghton was always racing him for money—big and strong enough to outmatch those Indian ponies.

"You think you can outrun those Indians if we can spring you loose?"

Houghton's long face sobered. "Yes, sir. Ain't

no horse ever caught Red once he was in front."

"I want you to carry a message to Captain Austin. You'll have to run that line of snipers below. We'll try to pin them down long enough. Once you're clear, I doubt any Indian pony will trouble you. Those snipers don't have ponies under their white skins, so you will only have to worry about the others, and you should have a good jump."

Corporal Houghton licked his lips. This was going to be a different kind of race, with a lot more than a month's pay on the line. "Uh . . . when do you want me to go, sir?"

Lieutenant Schaefer regarded the skinny corporal as if he had never seen him before. They were almost the same age, he thought. He knew little about Houghton, and he suddenly wished he knew more. This was what command came down to. It wasn't sitting up on a bluff and picking off fleeing Indians on their ponies, like shooting ducks from a blind. It was sending a skinny soldier out to risk his life because that was what he, Lieutenant Ernest Schaefer, had decided.

"Now, Corporal," he said quietly. "Move!"

Schaefer directed a heavy fire at the snipers in the creek as Corporal Houghton broke out of the wagon box on the run. He kept up the firing until the big bay gelding was well past the last known sniper.

There was a sudden silence within the square

when Schaefer ordered cease fire. Every man, trooper and civilian alike, watched the racing horse and rider receding in the distance, black against the endless expanse of white, until Houghton vanished over a ridge.

Puzzled, Lieutenant Schaefer turned to stare toward the main body of Indians, hidden beyond the stand of trees to the north and west. They didn't even try to stop him, he thought. They let him go. Why?

He could not know that this was also according to Draws-Out-Arrows' plan.

26

The confrontation between Crosswhite and Sut Rossiter held, rigid as hunting dogs at point, under the threat of the three armed troopers Captain Austin had left while he conferred with the rider from the wagons.

He returned on the run. "You'll have a chance to use your guns," he called out as he neared them. "Indians have attacked the wagons!"

"What?" The cry was Hubbard's.

"We'll ride at once," Captain Austin ordered. "Your men will follow, Mr. Hubbard."

There was an instant's hesitation. Then Hubbard said, "No, sir."

Austin, already turning away, swung back to face him. "What do you mean, Mr. Hubbard?"

"We're going on. I can't turn back now."

"Those are your wagons my men are guarding, Mr. Hubbard," the captain said angrily. "And some of your own men are also under siege. You can't mean to abandon them."

"I'm sure your soldiers can handle the Indians," Leland Hubbard said coldly. "That's what you're here for, Captain. But I mean to claim the prize I've journeyed all this way to find. You can't expect me to abandon *that*."

Austin glared at him. "I'm beginning to know

what to expect of you, Mr. Hubbard," he said with open contempt. "Very well then. I can't wait for you. Mr. Crosswhite? You're with us?" The question made unspoken but pointed reference to the fight Austin had prevented.

Crosswhite looked at him steadily. It was a way out, he thought, a way to save his hide. Without Austin and his troopers there would be no one to stop Sut Rossiter. In a sense Crosswhite would stand alone against Rossiter, Hubbard, and his entire crew.

But he spoke without hesitation. "I'll catch up, Captain. I've some unfinished business here."

Austin stared. "I don't know the reasons for your quarrel with Mr. Rossiter—"

"That's right, Captain. It's between us."

"I can't force you to leave with us," Austin said, still sounding angry. "I hope you know what you're doing."

"You'd best start riding," Crosswhite said. "I'll see you shortly."

"I hope so, Mr. Crosswhite. I sincerely hope so."

The young officer glared once more at Leland Hubbard. Then, without any further word, he strode to his waiting horse, mounted, and cantered over to the head of his assembled detachment. He did not look back.

Lee Crosswhite listened to the creak and rattle and chink of the mounted troopers until the sounds had died away, leaving behind a stillness that seemed to be made only deeper by the wind gusting across the frozen plain. He continued to watch Sut Rossiter. With all this waiting, his hands were stiff with cold, he thought, flexing his fingers. But Rossiter's would be as cold. The gunman had removed his gloves at the beginning of the calldown.

Rossiter showed his teeth. He's almost licking his chops, Crosswhite thought. "You had your chance to run," Rossiter said. "I'm surprised you didn't grab it."

"A man don't run from a sidewinder."

The white teeth vanished. "Show me what you do, drifter."

"Hold it!" Leland Hubbard's whipcrack command froze the coiling tension in Rossiter's body. "Roget could be wrong about finding that canyon easily. And we can't be dead sure Mr. Crosswhite has told us all he knows, or even spoken truthfully always. You're going with us, Mr. Crosswhite, like it or not."

"No."

"You can't fight a dozen guns."

Sut Rossiter was scowling. He didn't like being put off again. And Crosswhite had no greater relish for the prospect of riding with Rossiter behind him, even if he had been willing to lead Hubbard any closer to his prize. It had to be here, he thought.

"You told me he was mine," Rossiter growled.

"And I spoke the truth," Hubbard answered agreeably. "All in good time, Mr. Rossiter. Just make sure he rides with us for another hour. How you do it is not important to me."

The white-haired impresario turned away, but Crosswhite saw that several of his men remained alert and watchful, their hands close to their guns or, in one instance, holding a rifle ready.

Rossiter's mocking smile reappeared as he advanced slowly toward Crosswhite. "You gonna go easy, drifter, or do you want to make me work for it?"

"You had it easy one time," Crosswhite said softly.

So it wasn't to be guns, he thought. Not yet. And the others would let them fight without interfering. Warily he watched Rossiter to see which way his weight shifted. He saw the toes digging into the packed snow, warning him just before Rossiter charged.

He ducked under a roundhouse swing, straightening up with his feet planted solidly. He drove his fist into Sut Rossiter's face with all of his weight behind the blow. The big gambler was caught moving into the punch. It lifted him inches off his feet. He landed on wobbly legs and struggled to right himself. The grin was gone. For a brief moment his eyes rolled upward, almost disappearing under the lids.

Crosswhite was fairly certain he had broken a bone in his right hand. He had hit Rossiter as hard as he'd ever hit anyone or anything in his life.

And the big man was still standing.

Stepping in swiftly, Crosswhite landed two more solid blows, one to the chest and the other to the mouth, but he didn't swing as hard with his left arm, perhaps still favoring his shoulder. And Rossiter was falling away from the second blow, and he rode it out.

He should have gone down, Crosswhite thought. He was unable to close his right hand into a fist. A tingling pain ran up the arm into his shoulder like a message along the singing wires.

He was going to have to fight Rossiter with one hand again, just like the time in the bunkhouse.

The big man's eyes had cleared. He shook his head. Blood smeared his mouth. There was no mistaking the killing rage in those eyes now. Not even Leland Hubbard would stop him.

Favoring his right side as he had once favored the left, Crosswhite feinted a wild swing and followed the maneuver fast, driving his head and shoulder into Rossiter's middle. Rossiter was not fooled by the feint. He saw that something was wrong with Crosswhite's right hand and arm. He was stepping back when Crosswhite drove into him, and he was able to lock both arms around Crosswhite's body as they fell together.

Sut Rossiter rolled on top. He wrenched a hand free and tried to hook one of Crosswhite's eyes with his thumb. Evading this and twisting away, Crosswhite took an elbow in his throat.

He doubled over, choking soundlessly, his throat locked in agony. Those brief seconds were long enough for Rossiter to scramble to his feet and smash his boot into Crosswhite's ribs.

Raw pain seared his chest, burning flesh like scalding water. He had thought those ribs well healed, but they were still tender. He tried to get away from Rossiter's punishing boots, but they seemed to come from every direction, moving a lot faster than he could crawl.

Not gonna crawl, he thought dully. Are you gonna let him make you crawl a second time?

Another boot looped toward his face. His hands wouldn't move fast enough to grab it. All he could do was lift a shoulder, heaving upward. The shoulder took the force of the kick and pushed Rossiter's leg higher than he had anticipated. His other foot slipped on the snow. He went down like a big tree falling. Crosswhite watched him topple, slowly at first, then with gathering speed and force. He crashed onto his back with an impact that exploded air from his open mouth.

Slowly Crosswhite struggled erect. His left shoulder now shared the agony in his bruised ribs and his aching right hand. Sut Rossiter was writhing on the ground, his face purple with the struggle to breathe. His feet pushed feebly at the show, creating small piles. Crosswhite watched him with something like curiosity, as if he were detached from the scene, a bystander. When he heard the raw moaning in Rossiter's lungs that told him the big man was beginning to suck in air, he stepped thoughtfully on Rossiter's left hand, which was pressed against the ground for support, the fingers splayed out. That evens things, he said. He was surprised when no words sounded aloud. But Rossiter yelped in pain.

Carefully Crosswhite kicked him in the ribs.

He was beginning to feel stronger. He was recovering from the punishing effects of Rossiter's early kicks. On the other hand, Rossiter retained a gray look around his jowls. To his surprise Crosswhite saw that one of those large white teeth was missing, giving Rossiter a center point opening and changing his grimace into something comical. Maybe that's what he had hurt his hand on, Crosswhite thought. The discovery made him feel even better.

He waited for Rossiter to push himself off the snow. "I want you standin'," Crosswhite said in a matter-of-fact way.

When Rossiter was standing on his feet, swaying, Crosswhite knocked him down again.

The next time Rossiter managed to evade his blow and to land one of his own in return. Crosswhite skidded on his shoulder blades, surprised to find himself knocked flat. He was barely quick enough to escape those swinging boots.

Only when he was standing again did he marvel at the clumsiness of Rossiter's kicks. He saw that a new emotion lived beside the rage in Rossiter's eyes: fear. Rossiter knew that he should have been able to keep Crosswhite down. His kicks had been slow and clumsy and weak. With each shift of weight he staggered.

Now he was trying to evade Crosswhite's rushes, hardly making any real attempt to hit back. He tried to trap Crosswhite with a sudden bull's charge, head lowered. Crosswhite sidestepped the blind lunge, caught Rossiter by one shoulder and the seat of his pants, and threw him flat on his face.

He had acted instinctively, without thinking. And he had used both hands.

The right one wasn't broken after all. The pain was something he could live with.

He placed his right hand, testing it, on the back of Rossiter's head and shoved his face deeper into the snow. There was strong temptation to jump up and land with both feet in the small of Rossiter's defenseless back, stomping his spine. Instead he stepped back to wait.

"Get up," he croaked in an unrecognizable voice. "Get up, you cheatin' coyote. We're gonna count your teeth."

Rossiter took a long time rising. He was doubled over at the waist, and when he reached his feet he had his back toward Crosswhite as if he were blindly searching for him. Crosswhite knew then that he had won, that Rossiter was whipped—and that Rossiter believed it, too.

When Rossiter swung around to face him, his gun was in his hand.

Later Crosswhite was not sure exactly how the rest of it happened. He jumped back in surprise as the dark barrel of the six-shooter swung level. His feet slipped on the treacherous snow and skidded from under him. Rossiter's gun blazed. The flame seemed to leap directly in front of Crosswhite's eyes, but the shot passed over him as he went sprawling.

He rolled frantically in the snow, clawing at his hip with clumsy fingers. His right hand was still awkward, nerveless. He hooked the butt of the gun with the slot between thumb and palm. It slid clear, but he lost control of it. As he fumbled for it, another shot thundered in his ears.

Crosswhite waited for the brutal kick, the searing pain. Baffled when it failed to strike him, he searched for Sut Rossiter and found him, weaving on his feet, eyes wild, fifteen feet away. Rossiter tried to steady his right hand with the left, like a boy who finds a gun too heavy to hold.

Crosswhite's thick fingers closed on his six-shooter. He rolled again, shifting the gun from

217

his right hand to the left, finding sensitivity there, fingers cold but still able to grip.

Rossiter's third shot burned a crease in his right buttock as it passed over him. Lying flat on his belly, left elbow planted on the ground, Crosswhite took aim. There was snow clinging to his bloody lips and curtaining his eyelids. It was like shooting through the icy frost on a window at a figure blurred and wavering.

He was almost surprised to feel the gun kick in his hand. Through the frosty lace over his eyes he saw the same surprise mirrored in Sut Rossiter's face. Rossiter's mouth was open in a gap-toothed grin that suddenly pulled taut as a rope.

The impact of the bullet that struck Rossiter high in the chest lifted him up and flung his big body backward, weightless as a straw man blown from his stick by a gust of wind. Crosswhite watched him flounder across the snow. One of Rossiter's legs seemed to have an independent life of its own. It kicked at the frozen ground. Then the gunman flopped, straw body slack inside his greatcoat. He didn't seem to throw up any snow when he landed on his back, as if all substance as well as soul had fled.

Lee Crosswhite's arm dropped, the Colt heavy in his hand. Leland Hubbard's bellow of rage meant nothing to him at first. He gathered himself together very slowly, as if from a deep sleep. He was bruised and spent, almost too tired to stand.

Kneeling, he found his legs heavy, lifeless as stumps.

He picked up the Colt once more and looked up at Leland Hubbard. "You!" he said. The thought was not fully formulated, an accusation that had not taken shape, but it came out sounding like a threat.

"Shoot him!" Hubbard screamed.

Too late Crosswhite saw the double-barreled Remington derringer in Vorec's hand, pointing at his chest. His hand reached out in a kind of mute protest toward the dwarf, who had circled to Hubbard's left and was no more than a dozen feet away, standing stubby as a powder keg, his short legs braced wide.

The crash of the derringer and the blow of the .41-caliber slug were instantaneous. A great weight smashed into Crosswhite's chest. It spun him around and slammed him to the frozen ground. His head bounced hard. There was a roaring in his ears, tumultuous as an avalanche thundering down the steep walls of a canyon to bury him. His shout of pain and protest was lost in the uproar as a wall of white fury engulfed him. It clotted his eyes and mouth and nose. It pounded him downward under layers that turned from white to red to black. For a moment only pain and anguish penetrated that blackness like icy shards. Then there was nothing.

27

He woke to a silence deeper and colder than any he had ever known. The dream—or was it a dream?—of being buried under an avalanche returned as his mind groped toward awareness. Sudden terror constricted his throat. He *was* buried. A strange weight blanketed him completely, smothering him, blotting out all sound and light.

In his panic he tried to move. A savage pain tore at his left side.

But he saw light.

Pawing snow away from his face, Crosswhite peered into a gloom that was still daylight, the sky darkened by a screen of whirling snow. Relief opened the gates to a joy that filled his brain and sang in his blood. He was alive!

He lay still, letting the joy of life pulse through him—and mindful, too, of that raw pain when he tried to move.

He remembered Sut Rossiter flopping in the snow, and then—Vorec.

He hadn't expected Leland Hubbard to go so far. To take advantage of Rossiter's hatred and turn it to savings, yes, that was understandable in a greedy man. But with Rossiter dead, why order Vorec to shoot? Out of fear for his own skin, afraid that Crosswhite would hold him to account?

It made sense, Crosswhite thought. Hubbard probably would have preferred to keep Crosswhite alive until White Wolf's body was found, but he had chosen not to risk that choice after the fight with Rossiter erupted into a deadly gun battle. Besides, Roget had assured him he could find the canyon at the foot of the pink bluffs. Better gamble on that than on Crosswhite's unpredictable wrath.

He opened his eyes again—realizing that they had closed involuntarily while he reflected—to the steadily falling snow. How long had it been coming down? How long had he been unconscious? The gray skies and snow made it impossible to tell what time of day it was, but with winter closing in, the days were short, and it had been well past noon when the last of Hubbard's bottles of champagne had been emptied. An hour or so, he thought, maybe less.

The snow was piled several inches deep around his body, but that could be deceptive. New snow often looked deeper than it was, teased into currents and drifts by the wind, building up against immovable objects, like a body on the ground.

Sudden wonder—close to alarm—snapped his head up, bringing sharp pain to his head as well as his side. He searched out Sut Rossiter's body, featureless under a mantle of white. Dead, then. No lucky near-miss like the one that had left Crosswhite breathing.

The new snow was less than an inch deep in level areas. But it was descending with a steadiness that suggested there would be high and dangerous drifts before too many more hours had passed.

And no tracks to follow.

But he was alive. The pain was endurable. His fingers traced the stickiness of blood in his hair and then along the left side of his rib cage. Cautiously he opened his coat, seeing the hole where the bullet had burned through.

He lay back to let an attack of dizziness pass. The bullet hadn't knocked him out, he thought, it was that crack on the head when it struck the frozen ground. And the blow had probably saved his life. It had opened a cut that must have bled profusely and visibly, deceiving Hubbard and his "man" into believing that the shot had hit him in the head.

He probed further. The blood on his shirt had stiffened into dark ice. From lying against the packed snow, he thought. And the new snow had covered him like a blanket, warming him, keeping him from freezing.

A bullet of that caliber, fired from that distance, would have done a lot more damage if it had come from a larger weapon. His stiff fingers—he would be lucky if he escaped serious frostbite in his right hand, but the left had been pinned next to his body, warmed by it—gingerly examined the wound in his side. The slug had glanced off his ribs, lacking the velocity to penetrate at so sharp an angle. Torn skin, a bloody but shallow bite to match the furrow plowed across the seat of his pants by Rossiter's wild shot.

All in all, he had no right to be feeling as good as he did.

A languor stole over him. Best lie here until he was found, he thought. It hurt too much to move, and his body was too heavy to move anyway. Captain Austin would be coming along. . . .

He jerked awake, chilled by fear. If he slept, he would not wake again. With this snow falling as it was, Austin would never find him except by pure chance. That was too much luck to place his chips on. Not when they were the last chips in his pile.

Crosswhite forced himself to sit up, rubbing his hands, ignoring the assorted pains in head and body, telling himself that the pain eased as he moved about. His mind was beginning to work more clearly, weighing what had happened, assessing his chances to survive after being shot and abandoned.

Better than Hubbard's chances of finding White Wolf, he thought with satisfaction. Roget might have led Hubbard to that canyon on a clear day, but he would soon be lost in this snow, which created new patterns and perspectives. If Hubbard had any sense he would turn back to his wagons, hurrying to reach them before dark.

If he did, he would find Crosswhite riding to meet him.

Hatred had a way of widening and deepening its path, as if it were too strong a passion to be controlled. What had been between him and Rossiter, a private quarrel, had now come to include Hubbard and Vorec.

Anger helped Crosswhite struggle to his feet—anger and the sharpening realization that his plight was more serious than he had yet faced. Obviously Hubbard had believed him dead. Equally obviously he would not have left the sorrel behind. A dead man's horse was fair game.

But he had!

Crosswhite heard the soft whinny of the horse before he saw it. Then a big shape materialized out of the falling snow, gray and tall, moving tentatively toward him.

His elation died. Not the sorrel. The claybank. Crosswhite had brought her along that morning partly because she carried his extra gear, partly because the determination to face Leland Hubbard and cut loose from his caravan was already half-formed, waiting only for the harsh truths he had pried out of Hubbard at the last.

Why hadn't Hubbard taken her? Most likely

she had given him or his men trouble. The sorrel would have gone meekly, more used to obedience, married to no one man in spite of her loyalty. The claybank would have pulled back and fought if she were approached too hastily or jerked too roughly.

Now the big horse stood motionless, a few feet away, watching him. Crosswhite stared at her in dismay. His situation was hardly better than being abandoned on foot in a storm. All he had was a horse who couldn't be ridden.

And he knew that he would not walk off this high table alive.

Hubbard hadn't even left him his gun.

He swung back toward Sut Rossiter's huddled shape. A slim possibility, but worth testing. He brushed snow away from the body. Rossiter lay face down, his right side under, as his body was half turned. No one had moved him. His left-side holster was empty, the ivory-handled Colt missing. But in their haste the searchers had forgotten Rossiter's second gun. Crosswhite slicked it out of its holster, wiped off the snow and ice particles, and shoved it into his own empty leather.

It would be enough to keep off the wolves for a while at least, if it came to that.

Thoughtfully he retraced his steps and came to the side of the claybank mare. She did a short sideways shuffle away from him, then stopped.

"You don't like this storm any more than I do, huh, girl?" he said aloud.

Slowly, cautiously, he reached out to take the trailing lines. The mare's ears flattened slightly, but she didn't break. He continued to talk to her, clucking soothingly and patting her neck.

"You wanta get out of this, girl, it has to be my way. Like it or not, that's the way it's gonna be." He walked her in slow circles until he found his hat, lost at the start of his fight with Rossiter. He slapped it against his thigh, sending snow flying.

If she threw him, that was trail's end, he thought, eyeing the blanket and roll on her back. Under any other circumstances he would no more have thought of climbing onto her bareback than he would have bedded down in a rattlesnake pit. But sometimes you couldn't choose where you slept or how you rode.

He felt the weakness in his arms and legs when he stood beside the mare. He'd never make it up, he thought.

He glanced back at Sut Rossiter's body.

There was no malice in his decision. Rossiter was dead, and the hatred Crosswhite felt had died with him. In retrospect it seemed strange that he could have felt so strongly, although he knew that under the same provocation he would feel the same again. Anger and hatred were like a sickness; it was hard to remember how bad it was once the fever had broken. So the use of

Rossiter's body as a step-up for mounting the claybank was an act not of contempt but of hard necessity. One way or another Crosswhite had to climb onto that ornery dun if he meant to stay alive.

She moved obediently enough on the lead, stopping at the soft pressure of Crosswhite's hands. He took a deep breath, gathering his strength, stepped up, and vaulted from Rossiter's back onto the mare's. His left hand dug into her mane. The numbed fingers of his right hand groped for another hold.

He felt a tremor pass through her body. The powerful muscles quivered like strummed wires. Hunching over her neck and tightening the grip of his knees, he endured his own body's protest at more punishment to come. He was bruised and cut and frostbitten, and only the cold had kept him from bleeding to death. And he was no Indian. Without saddle and stirrups he would need to sprout wings after the mare's first jump.

She took one stiff-legged step and stopped, still trembling.

"Jump, damn you," he muttered. "What's holdin' you now?"

The claybank gave a toss of her head and a soft snuffle in reply. Then she stamped one hoof a couple of times, pawing the snow.

"Hell's fire," Crosswhite breathed.

She was tamed. The weeks of trailing along on

the lead, of being fed and watered and stroked and talked to, had done what force had failed to accomplish.

"I never could figger out a filly," he told her, "but I won't question what made you change your mind. You picked a good time, is all."

He walked her in a gentle circle, letting her get used to his weight, continuing to talk to her, a slow elation warming his body and touching his cracked lips with a smile. At last he paused and knew that he had been postponing a choice he would not have had to make if the claybank had thrown him.

The cavalry might need help, but he didn't have to hunt for arguments that tempted him west instead of east, along Leland Hubbard's trail rather than Austin's. The odds were that Austin's troopers could handle what they faced better than Hubbard. The snowstorm had changed a lot of things. Hubbard, an Easterner, might not listen to wiser heads in his party about turning back in the face of the storm. He didn't know how quickly he and his crew could be isolated by the storm, how deadly it could be to be lost or trapped on this high plain in deep snow. Crosswhite had been over the ground twice now in recent weeks; the terrain was fresh in his mind. He would have a better chance of leading survivors back to the wagons than they would have on their own.

He knew that vengeance also tempted him. He

had something to settle with Hubbard and Vorec. He had to ask himself if that was why he wanted to follow them instead of the cavalry, and he was not sure of the answer.

He laid the reins gently across the claybank's proud neck, turning her west, clucking softly with his tongue.

It was no longer a matter of stopping Leland Hubbard, of preventing any defiling of White Wolf's body, or of revenge. If he didn't turn that party back, they would never return to their wagons alive.

An hour later, plodding directly into the wind, his head ducked to bring his hat brim between him and the blowing snow, he began to wonder if he was lost. There were no tracks—his own disappeared almost as soon as they were formed. Not even the mountains were visible to guide him. He should have *felt* their bulk by now even without seeing them.

It seemed darker, but he could not be sure. Maybe it was only that the snow was thicker, the wind blowing harder. He had lost all sense of time. There might be an hour or two of light remaining, a little longer after that before full darkness made safe travel impossible in the storm.

He knew that he had to turn back soon or be trapped alone.

It made no sense to go on. Hubbard had chosen his own path. The others hadn't been forced to follow him. They had all willingly left Crosswhite to die in the snow.

No, that wasn't certain. They had believed him dead. They had had no real choice but to go after Hubbard. What prizes, what rewards had he used to lure them all? They were no worse than Crosswhite, no more guilty or criminally inclined, no more deserving to die.

He grinned, showing his teeth to the teeth of the storm. He had wanted a safe refuge for the winter, Annie had charged. Well, he'd certainly picked a fine one, tracking a man he didn't like into a blizzard to save a pack of greedy men, not one of whom he could call friend.

Some of them should have known better than to go on once the snow began to come down heavily. Roget, for one. What kind of scout—

Crosswhite pulled up. Something had moved in the thicket of snow ahead. Was that a shout he'd heard? Or a scream?

Then he saw him—a small, grotesque figure, stumbling and falling as he ran through the snow. No, Crosswhite thought, shock jolting him and driving his one good hand toward Rossiter's white-handled gun. The figure in the snow was Vorec, but he was not running. He was at the end of a rope. He was being dragged.

The other end of the line had been invisible. Now

a larger shape rode out of the curtain of snow—
an Indian pony. Astride it, wearing a magnificent fur-collared greatcoat—Leland Hubbard's
coat—was a painted and feathered Indian warrior.

The Indian stopped. For an instant he and
Crosswhite faced each other through the heavy
fall of snow that swirled around them, as if both
men were too astonished to react.

Then Crosswhite's left hand closed on the butt
of the six-shooter and dragged it clear.

28

Draws-Out-Arrows had been puzzled by the purpose of the white men's expedition ever since his scouts had brought first news of the appearance of an escorted caravan traveling north. He had kept his distance, staying within the protection of the hills to the west, content to watch and wait until he knew the enemy's destination.

Two days passed. During that time he cautioned his scouts to be as invisible as the wind, while never losing sight of the enemy. By late afternoon of that second day, however, Skan the sky had darkened, as if in anger or displeasure. The wind quickened, and there was a heaviness in the air that foretold the coming of a storm.

His scouts had reported the presence of a white-haired leader of the white-eyes, a man who rode a magnificent horse and slept in a white man's tipi. Unquestionably he was a great chief, perhaps even one of those who came from Washington with empty promises.

It would be fitting, Draws-Out-Arrows thought, if this White Hair's scalp would replace the spirit of his dead brother.

But a storm might cause the white-eyes to turn back. They feared the wind and the snow.

And once they turned away there would be no opportunity for vengeance.

It was then that the first phase of his plan was born. When the enemy camped beside the creek, drawing their wagons into a protective square, he remained curious over their mission. His hope was to provoke the cavalry escort into taking action, drawing the pony soldiers away from the wagons and the remaining whites. While some of his braves lured the bluecoats into a long chase, leading away from the camp, Draws-Out-Arrows and others of his band would attack the camp and invade the tipi of the long-haired one.

After darkness he sent two brave scouts into the enemy camp. They were to attempt to steal horses, but Draws-Out-Arrows did not care if they succeeded in this. The act itself would be a challenge the pony soldiers could not ignore. In the morning, surely, they would set out to find their enemy.

His scouts performed their duty with courage and cunning. Each earned a new feather for the killing of the sentry and the successful invasion of the camp, an action meant to puzzle and frighten the white soldiers.

Would the bluecoats respond? Would White Hair lead them into battle?

In the morning white scouts followed the tracks of the two warriors until losing them. Draws-Out-Arrows was hopeful that his maneuver had succeeded. The scouts returned to their camp, and Draws-Out-Arrows waited.

Soon, as he had hoped, there was activity in the camp, and many of the white-eyes rode west, leaving a smaller number, about fifteen men, to protect the wagons. The others, including twenty of the bluecoats, rode with the white-haired chief and others of his followers. This force was as large as Draws-Out-Arrows' entire band—larger if he deployed some of his men to watch or harass the camp beside the creek.

He had to find a way to divide the enemy's force once more.

At a safe distance he followed the enemy as they rode toward the mountains. Still puzzled by their mysterious mission, for they no longer seemed to be hunting an enemy in the field but were moving purposefully westward, Draws-Out-Arrows continued to ponder a way to trick the hated *wasicu*.

Then the second phase of his plan of attack leaped into his mind, complete in all its details, so clear that he felt an awed conviction that the plan was not his at all but had been borne to him on the wind.

If the white camp were attacked, and a scout brought this news, some of the soldiers would have to turn back. Perhaps, if the expedition's goal was important enough, the white-haired leader would go on. There was a possibility that the enemy's numbers would thus be split again.

Whichever group proceeded west—he could only believe that the plan that had been delivered to him was a good one, and how could it be otherwise?—would be small enough to attack.

Wounded Heel, who had lately received many honors, was chosen to return to the camp along the creek with a small band of followers. His duty was to attack and contain the enemy at the camp, with one exception: He was to permit a scout to ride unmolested if one was sent from the camp.

Draws-Out-Arrows was quite certain the scout would come. White Wolf, his brother, had schooled him in the ways of the pony soldiers and other *wasicu.* They did not desire to fight bravely in small groups. They had learned better than the Indians—better than the Sioux nation of brothers—to fight together, winning battles by the sheer weight of their numbers. It was a lesson, White Wolf had said, that the Indians had learned well in the battle along the banks of the Little Big Horn. But it had come too late.

At midday White Hair and his followers surprised him by stopping in the middle of the plain to enjoy a feast. What were they cele-brating? Draws-Out-Arrows could not approach closer without risk of detection, but he was made uneasy by this feast. It suggested a belief in good medicine on the part of White Hair.

Worriedly, Draws-Out-Arrows thought of the

very small man who rode closer to White Hair, a strange figure half the size of a warrior. Did this one also carry magic?

But before the feast had ended a lone rider from the east was seen by one of Draws-Out-Arrows' own scouts. The camp was under attack, and the rider brought a plea for help.

Satisfied, Draws-Out-Arrows waited. His medicine was good. He knew now that White Hair would continue westward toward the mountains. The gods had decreed that it would be so.

Shots were heard from the enemy camp, but their meaning was unknown. This could be part of the mysterious celebration, he thought. But he was more concerned about the storm that was now clearly visible over the mountains and moving toward them. Would White Hair fear the storm? Would it cause him to turn back?

But all went as he had hoped. The pony soldiers separated from White Hair and his other followers and rode at great speed in the direction of their camp. Draws-Out-Arrows sent one scout to follow them, making certain that the action of the bluecoats was not a trick designed to lure him into a trap. With the main body of his own band, which now outnumbered White Hair and his men by almost two to one, he began to stalk the enemy, edging closer as the sky darkened and the storm drew near.

And at last he knew that the bluecoats had

indeed ridden to relieve the defenders of the wagons. There had been no trick.

This was to be a day of battle, of honor and great deeds, and the spirit of his brother would once more know the joy of victory.

It began to snow. Tracking was at once more difficult and safer. It no longer mattered that White Hair might decide to turn back. He would not escape.

The small enemy force neared the mountains. Scouts rode out ahead of the party, searching. For what? The initial puzzle remained: What had brought White Hair and his followers toward these hills in the face of the storm? Was it the glittering metal? What else did the white man prize so highly?

White Hair's scout rode back in haste. The bearded leader called his men into a circle and spoke to them. Hidden by a shallow flank of the low foothills near the mountains, Draws-Out-Arrows was close enough now to admire White Hair's fine horse and to hear the distant thunder of his voice. Crazy Horse had spoken with such a voice, and his brother White Wolf had spoken thus, in a voice to awaken the sleeping courage in any warrior.

With satisfaction that did not quite eliminate his surprise, Draws-Out-Arrows watched the enemy ride toward a deep canyon whose walls wore the color of the sun on the horizon. White

Hair was completely without fear, without guile. The clarity of this truth made Draws-Out-Arrows uneasy, almost afraid. White Hair scorned even to look for an enemy nearby. He had supreme confidence in the power of his medicine. Why else would he ride into the mouth of a canyon from which there was no escape—like an eagle circling the baited trap?

Draws-Out-Arrows leaped onto his waiting pony. He pulled himself proudly erect so that all of his followers might see. The brave White Wolf had not been afraid. Neither was his brother.

Only when the white-eyes were very close to the opening of the canyon did Draws-Out-Arrows discover that there was something ahead of them—a figure in the branches of a tree. White Hair's horse galloped ahead of the others toward the tree. What magic was this?

Again Draws-Out-Arrows felt a touch of wonder and fear. Again he thrust it aside with stubborn defiance. He had sworn to avenge his brother's death. He would not abandon that promise in disgrace.

Quickly he sent warriors on foot to climb the canyon walls on both sides. He was left with a dozen mounted men—an equal number to White Hair and his followers. From his high ground Draws-Out-Arrows waited until he heard the soft hooting of an owl. His lightly clad snipers—they had shed their robes, no longer needing them, warmed by the fires of courage—were in place among the rocky cliffs, flanking the enemy, although the falling snow now hid them from his sight. White Hair by this time had reached the tall tree he had sought. His followers were gathered around him.

Draws-Out-Arrows pushed the puzzle away from his mind. Soon there would be answers. Now he rode at the head of his warriors, carrying his lance and one of the fine pony-soldier rifles that would speak many times without being reloaded. He left the higher ground and could no longer see White Hair and his men. He came to the tracks the enemy had made in the fresh snow—tracks already filling in as the storm descended with increasing fury.

Visibility was now poor. No matter. Draws-Out-Arrows rode directly toward the mouth of the canyon, following the wide trail made by White Hair and his men. The whirling snow shielded the Indians until they were very close to the enemy.

Until the trap had closed.

One of White Hair's scouts had climbed onto the lower branches of the tall pine. The others all watched him avidly. The man in the tree looked up—and saw the approaching Indians. His warning shout was almost lost in the smothering snow flurries.

Draws-Out-Arrows waited no longer. With a

shrill and menacing whoop he urged his pony into a run. Around him his warriors took up the cry. And from the walls of the canyon came the crackle of rifle fire.

The white-eyes wheeled around in panic and confusion, blundering into each other. A sniper's bullet struck the man who crouched in the tree, and he plummeted to the ground. Through the gunfire and the war cries and the whistling of the wind, Draws-Out-Arrows heard White Hair's bellow of rage. The roar of a huge bear attacked. Valiantly the Indian rode straight at him.

The sudden fury of the attack demoralized the enemy. On foot and on horseback they scattered in fear. Immediately the Indians were among them, shooting and striking with lance and tomahawk. A few of the white-eyes turned to fight. More than one warrior spilled from his pony as the enemy's rifles spoke death. The puffs of smoke from the guns were invisible in the falling snow, which seemed to thicken at the bottom of the canyon as if its walls contained and intensified the storm in the way rocks will enclose a fire.

Draws-Out-Arrows had eyes only for White Hair. At every moment he expected the white chief to leap toward him with a great warrior's courage and ferocity.

But the white-haired, white-bearded leader with a face as red as an Indian's wheeled away from Draws-Out-Arrows' charge and turned his powerful horse down the canyon.

Astonished, Draws-Out-Arrows pursued him. Was it a trick at last? Or didn't White Hair know that the canyon was a box without a door?

The confusion of battle fell quickly behind the two enemies, muffled by the storm. Through layers of snow as thick as smoke, Draws-Out-Arrows saw his enemy rein in his horse frantically, skidding to a stop in a cascade of snow as a steep wall confronted him. He looked around wildly.

It was no trick. White Hair had fled in fear. Contempt curled the Indian's lips as he rode to the attack. Swinging around, White Hair saw him closing swiftly. He held up his arm, palm extended in mute protest or plea. His face was red and swollen. He did not even try to fight.

Draws-Out-Arrows squeezed the trigger of his rifle when he was no more than a dozen strides from the enemy. The bullet struck White Hair in the chest. His great horse reared in panic as he toppled from the saddle. The horse bolted away from Draws-Out-Arrows, dragging his fallen rider across the snow-covered floor of the canyon. A moment later the walls pinched inward. The horse stopped, baffled, and at last stood motionless.

Draws-Out-Arrows rode close. He stared down at the enemy, now proven a coward. But he was the leader of the white-eyes. His craven flight did not change that.

The Indian slipped from his pony. With a quick twist he freed the fallen man's boot from the stirrup, and his horse danced away.

White Hair's eyes, bright blue as the sky in summer, were open wide, staring up at the paint-daubed face of his enemy. He was still alive. Draws-Out-Arrows seized his knife. He spoke harshly. Thus did he avenge his brave brother, leader of the Lakotas. Thus did he keep his pledge.

He knelt in a fluid motion. His knife flashed. White Hair screamed.

The scream cut off, severed like a cord.

Draws-Out-Arrows worked quickly with his knife. Seconds later he stood proudly, holding the trophy he had sworn to gain, the spirit-hair by which White Wolf was both avenged and reborn to him.

A cry that was both exultation and grief burst from the Indian's throat. Then he was silent.

When he rode back along the canyon he wore the fine fur coat White Hair had owned. The enemy's superb horse trailed behind his own.

The battle was over. All of the enemy had been killed, surely, for the victorious warriors were now gathered around the tree where the enemy had been surprised. A way was made for Draws-Out-Arrows as he approached. As he reached the tree he saw two things, equally astonishing. On the ground was one of the enemy, the small man he had seen only from a distance, a remarkable figure who would come only to Draws-Out-Arrows' waist if they stood together. His startling appearance, with his stubby bowed legs and his large head, was the only reason he was still alive, for it had made his captors uncertain, more than a little frightened. If he were killed, might his strange magic not haunt his enemies, somehow shrinking and diminishing them?

The second discovery was even more stunning. In the branches of the tree, laid out as if on a burial scaffold, was his brother, White Wolf.

For a long time Draws-Out-Arrows stared at his brother. How had he come here? Who had placed him there in the branches of the tree, protected by thick brush?

And at last Draws-Out-Arrows saw that here was a greater magic than any man could understand. White Wolf had chosen this place to die. Through some mystery of the spirit world he had lured the white-haired chief to this spot—and to his death. The plan that had come to Draws-Out-Arrows on the wind was not his own inspiration but White Wolf's magic, reaching out beyond the time of his dying to strike one final blow against his hated enemy, the enemy who had stolen his land and the pride of his people.

Draws-Out-Arrows was filled with wonder. He

looked down at the small man crouching terrified near the base of the tree, where thorny bare branches poked and cut him. The Indian felt no fear. No enemy medicine could touch him while he was in the presence of White Wolf's great magic.

He alighted and strode toward the cowering dwarf, who cringed from him. Draws-Out-Arrows reached down and touched him with his hand.

Smiling, he turned to his followers. "There is nothing to fear," he said.

He beckoned the others forward. All would touch the dwarf while the entire band witnessed the coup, the act of courage.

Every man did as Draws-Out-Arrows bade. Some were frightened, but they did not hang back. It was a moment that would be recounted for many winters to come, and that would give a name to this battle and this time: the winter of the coup.

When it was over, Draws-Out-Arrows seized a rope taken from White Hair's horse and threw it over the dwarf, catching his head and one arm and shoulder in its loop. He jerked it tight. Then he mounted his pony and walked it in widening circles, dragging the little man behind, proving his courage and defiance of the white man's magic. The dwarf stumbled often and fell, but each time Draws-Out-Arrows dragged him through the snow until he regained his feet.

The snow was now very thick, so thick in falling that the dwarf at the end of the rope was almost invisible at times. In that storm there was no sound but the keening of the wind. Draws-Out-Arrows did not hear the approaching rider until he looked up and saw him just a few steps away.

For an instant they stared at each other in surprise. That moment was long enough for Draws-Out-Arrows to realize that the pony-soldiers had returned, that this was surely one of their scouts riding ahead.

He saw the scout reach for his gun. Draws-Out-Arrows dropped the rope, releasing the child-sized enemy, and immediately vanished into the storm.

In such a snowstorm the bluecoats would not be able to follow or attack them successfully. He rejoined his waiting warriors and spoke quickly, urgently. He took the red-streaked patch of long white hair he had won from the enemy, and with a few twists attached the hair to his lance. With a proud arrogance he held it high.

"We have won the victory," he said. "We have kept our pledge. White Wolf is avenged, and his spirit once more rides with us."

Now they could withdraw with honor.

29

When the Indian in warpaint disappeared into what seemed like a solid wall of snow, Lee Crosswhite was still struggling to cope with his borrowed six-shooter, awkwardly using his left hand. He let out a puff of relief, his cheeks blowing. Lucky he didn't want to fight no more than I did, he thought.

Luck. He'd thought a lot about luck lately. In a way all that thinking about fortune, the bad and the good, had brought him here. A man could get to thinking too much entirely about how lucky or unlucky he was. And he'd either start feeling sorry for himself, as Crosswhite had, or he'd begin thinking he was somebody special, favored of the gods. Maybe that was what Leland Hubbard had believed.

Crosswhite knew that the entrepreneur from the East was dead. He didn't know why it had happened, and that might never be known, but that Indian in his warpaint had been a triumphant Indian. He hadn't run because he was scared but because he didn't need to win any more honor this day.

All this while Vorec had been kneeling on the ground, covered with snow, entangled in a rope, staring at Crosswhite with evident fear. As worried about me as he was about that Indian, Crosswhite guessed.

Strangely, he felt no animosity toward the stubby man now, in spite of the gunshot wound in his side. Vorec had been Hubbard's man right up to the end. He'd only been doing his duty. Nothing personal, mind you.

Vorec tried to scramble away when Crosswhite swung down from the claybank, but he hadn't been able to struggle out of the loop of the rope, and Crosswhite caught the trailing end of the line.

"You get lost in this snow and ain't nobody ever gonna find you," Crosswhite said mildly. "You got worse things to worry about than what I'm gonna do to you." If that sounded like a threat postponed, well, Vorec had earned a little worrying at least.

He loosened the lariat and set Vorec free. Not an Indian rope, he noted, confirming his hunch about Hubbard's fate. Not that he'd entertained any real doubts.

"Mr. Hubbard? Did they—?"

"Dead," Vorec cried in his high, rasping voice. "All of them! I don't know where they come from. They were like—"

"Uh huh. Savages." Crosswhite peered gloomily through the snow. Was the screen thinning slightly? Or was that only a wish? "They steal all the horses?"

"I . . . I don't know." Vorec looked up at him in anxious appeal. "Why didn't they kill me?"

Crosswhite hesitated. "You're different," he said. "Indians don't like to fool much with what they don't understand, or anyone strange. They'll leave a madman alone, and—"

"And a dwarf," Vorec said bitterly, as if he regretted being alive when he might have joined the others in being massacred.

Briefly Crosswhite considered turning about and hightailing it eastward while he still had his hair, but he concluded that the Indians would have attacked before this if they were going to.

A quick search confirmed his hunch. Moreover, the Indians had left too hastily to find all of the horses in the confusion and the storm's poor visibility. Crosswhite and Vorec discovered three horses huddled together near some sheltering rocks at the base of a cliff. Still searching, calling out frequently to each other so that neither would become lost, they found only one other mount. It was Crosswhite's own sorrel gelding, still carrying his saddle.

Crosswhite lost no time switching from the claybank to the sorrel. He was hurting in enough places without having to ride bareback any longer.

Vorec found Hubbard's scalped corpse in the canyon beyond the pine where White Wolf's body had been laid to rest. The Indian was gone.

They had borne him away, safe from white vengeance or mutilation, a great chief returning in spirit to those among whom he had lived and fought, and won great honor.

The dwarf would not leave Hubbard. With great difficulty, Crosswhite and Vorec between them managed to heave Hubbard's body across the saddle of one of the recovered horses. Four other dead men were loaded onto the remaining mounts, including the claybank mare, after setting one horse aside for Vorec to ride. Someone would have to come back for the other bodies when the storm ended. That might be next spring, Crosswhite thought, although there were usually breaks in the weather this early in winter.

With lengths of rope he strung the horses together so that none would become separated. He rode at the head of the string, Vorec immediately behind him. He kept thinking about the tears he had seen in the little man's eyes when he knelt in the snow beside Leland Hubbard's body. The bond between them had been sealed with something more than greed. Who could understand it?

An hour later the snow had clearly begun to thin out, but the late afternoon was becoming increasingly dark. Crosswhite was wondering how far his new run of luck was going to carry him when he heard a shout and some muffled jingling of cavalry gear. Captain Austin, at the head of his detachment, rode out of the haze and hailed him delightedly.

They reached Chugwater Creek after dark. In the darkness they had wandered upstream, but once they blundered upon the creek they were able to follow its banks until they came to the wagons and their camp. There were signs that the force of the storm was dwindling. They would wait it out. They had makeshift shelter and plenty of food.

Together Austin and Crosswhite were able to piece together the Indians' maneuvering. The attack on the wagons had been a feint, intended to do exactly what it accomplished: draw Austin's troopers back to the wagons, leaving Hubbard and his crew alone in the field. As soon as Austin's relief had reached the wagons, the attacking Indians had melted away, evading pursuit.

Captain Arthur Austin reflected ruefully on the sobering lesson he had learned in Indian tactics. This discussion took place inside Austin's tent, which had been raised within the wagon box where it was somewhat protected from Indian attack and offered dubious shelter against the storm. Many of the troopers had found space either in the wagons or under them. Four others, including Lieutenant Ernest Schaefer, were crowded into the captain's tent along with Austin and Crosswhite.

Austin returned to the most puzzling aspect of the day's events. "How do you suppose they knew Hubbard was looking for White Wolf's body?"

"I don't see how they could've known what he was after," Crosswhite said slowly. "It's my guess they was followin' us, lookin' to make trouble. Don't forget they tried to steal our horses before we ever swung west to where I left that Indian."

"Still, it looks like a well-conceived plan," Austin insisted, reluctant to admit that an unlettered savage had outwitted him with improvised tactics. "This was a logical place for us to camp if wc intended to send a party toward the mountains. And they were waiting for Hubbard when he got there."

"It kinda looks like that."

Crosswhite guessed that they would never know for sure. Vorec had said that White Wolf's body was still in the tree when Hubbard reached it. Crosswhite found it unlikely that the Indians would have left the body there if they had discovered it themselves beforehand. It seemed more probable that they had trailed Hubbard and his crew, carrying out a planned act of vengeance. Hubbard had led them unexpectedly to the old chief's body.

"Well, you lost your reward, Mr. Crosswhite," Captain Austin commented after a while.

"But I suppose you're glad it's over all the same."

"Yeah."

They listened to the wind whipping tree branches overhead. In a corner of the tent one of the sleeping troopers was snoring. Young Lieutenant Schaefer was also asleep. He had acquitted himself well, by all reports, in his skirmish with the Indians. As had Austin, Crosswhite thought. The captain had kept his head, he had been quick to admit being fooled, and he had wasted no time in leading his troopers westward to search for Hubbard and his men. That action had come too late for Hubbard, but Crosswhite guessed that he and Vorec might owe their lives to the captain's cool decisiveness.

"It's ironic," Austin mused. "Mr. Hubbard losing his scalp that way. It's almost as if—"

"As if what, Captain?"

"Well, it's like poetic justice, Mr. Crosswhite. I mean, you could almost say that Hubbard was no better than that savage. In a way they were both after the same thing."

Crosswhite worked this over. After a moment he said, "That Indian ain't gonna sell tickets to the Queen of England," he said. "He didn't take that scalp for a circus, or to make money off it, like Mr. Hubbard had in mind. I reckon that's the difference. Guessin' that he's kin to White Wolf,

I'd say that Indian had better reason for takin' his trophy than Hubbard did."

Austin regarded him with curiosity. "Perhaps you're right at that. I hold no brief for Mr. Hubbard, dead or alive." Briefly he was silent. "The United States Army will not see it that way, of course. They won't let it go. They can't let it go. And the newspapers—" He shook his head. "That was a massacre, Mr. Crosswhite, a bloody massacre. And Mr. Hubbard was no ordinary man. He had—"

"I know. He had friends in Washington."

"Exactly."

Austin's face grew thoughtful, his eyes focusing on some distant point. Crosswhite guessed that he was thinking ahead to another winter campaign, tracking down the Indian renegades responsible for the massacre of the Hubbard party. He was a soldier, and he probably anticipated the campaign with some zest. Besides, the expedition had been his responsibility to protect, and he had failed in that. No doubt his superiors would hold him accountable, just as he had judged and found himself wanting.

"What will you do now, Mr. Crosswhite? That is, after we get you to a doctor and have you patched up."

"Wait for spring," he said. He thought of Annie Macauley's challenge. *Just come around in the spring and ask me that same question, Lee*

Crosswhite. Just so's I know you mean it. A slow grin cracked his lips. "Back to Cheyenne, and wait for spring."

"Yes." Captain Arthur Austin nodded absently, pulling his greatcoat tighter over his chest and reaching for a blanket. "It looks like a long winter, Mr. Crosswhite. A very long winter indeed."

Center Point Large Print
600 Brooks Road / PO Box 1
Thorndike, ME 04986-0001 USA

(207) 568-3717

US & Canada:
1 800 929-9108
www.centerpointlargeprint.com